Bobbie's Ants

Cherie Fruehan

ESSENTIAL ROCKSTAR, LLC.

BOBBIE'S ANTS

FIRST EDITION, MARCH 2026

EBook ISBN: 978-1-7346141-5-2

Trade Paperback ISBN: 978-1-7346141-4-5

Copy Edit: Penni Askew, Word Summit Editing

Book Design: Cherie Fruehan

For permissions contact author: www.cheriefruehan.com

This book is dedicated to anyone who has ever felt lonely, or like they didn't fit in.

In a universe so vast, we can't be the only ones…

1985

Worker ants travel, single file, through a network of complex tunnels meticulously excavated in fine sand, oblivious to the big blue orbs watching over them. The two moons of denim ringed with navy suspended over the tiny universe belong to the face of an awestruck child.

Bobbie Ann Broadbent pushes oversized glasses up her freckled nose, magnifying her eyes so large, they seem to fill the frames of her child-sized spectacles. Crystalline lakes bound by tortoiseshell rest on her copper, speckled cheeks.

Bobbie leans in close—close enough to fog the glass of her homemade ant farm.

"Sorry, folks, didn't mean to block your view," she says. And with the squee of a ten-year-old thumb, she swipes away breath from glass.

Bobbie lies on her bedroom floor in her solar system pj's, her face impossibly close to her farm, practically willing herself into the tiny environment. She yearns to be a part of the colony. An only child to a single mother, she longs for for family, for connection, for community—to shrink herself so small, she becomes one with her miniature friends.

She's certain her ants know her, every bit of her, more than anyone on earth. Maybe it's because she tells them everything. Even the things she's afraid to say out loud. She believes her ants can read her mind, and she's absolutely certain they understand.

Bobbie presses her nose to the glass and imagines she's one of the six-legged creatures, falling in line with the herd as they move over the soft terrain of a completely different planet. She imagines, once in their world, the ants rally around her—a little community of acceptance, working together, needing and relying on one another to survive.

From outside the glass, she marvels at their movements, timed and deliberate, directed by pheromones, keeping perfect rhythm. Like synchronized swimmers, they dance as one.

Ignored by most, ants are amazing creatures, and no one knows that better than Bobbie.

She sits up and scribbles on a drawing pad with crayons, chronicling what she sees. She carefully outlines big, black eyes shaped like apple seeds, and sketches reddish-brown bodies, disjointed into abstract shapes, coloring them with conviction.

Documenting her friends is something she does on a regular basis. All four of her bedroom walls are adorned with the creatures—tiny artworks, plastered as high as her hands can reach. Even while hoisted on tippy-toes, they barely make it halfway up the wall. Sketches of ants, haphazardly drawn—yet scientifically correct—paper every inch of her small room. On her desk, scrapbooks and binders, burst with more of the same.

But ants aren't her only passion. Bobbie's room is also filled with books about outer space. Picture books about planets and their constellations, inherited from her father's childhood collection, sit atop her small desk, fanned open to her favorite pages, their well-worn edges ruffled with wear. It's safe to say, Bobbie is a little science nerd.

With a shift of the wind, a sudden breeze blows through the open window above her desk, rustling the papers stuck to her wall and curling their corners like the fallen leaves of an old oak tree. The noise draws her attention to the windowpane with the night sky framed like a piece of art, as starry beacons twinkle over a bucolic countryside, silent and peaceful. As she scans the sky filled with familiar constellations, Bobbie wonders if her ants are as taken by the stars as she.

"Ten more minutes, Bobbie Ann," Norma Broadbent calls from the other room.

"Okay, Momma."

She doesn't want to go to bed. She never does—not when she was spending time with her favorite creatures. She felt they loved her too, that somehow, they knew she was a friend. She noticed her ants became more active when she talked to them, picking up their pace in their tiny world. This always made her giggle.

"Bobbie Ann…" her mother calls again.

"Rats," she whispers. She didn't want to. But, she was a good girl, and she knew enough to listen to her mother. "Okay, guys, Mom says it's time for—"

A *sonic boom* echoes outside the window as a simultaneous flash illuminates the unsuspecting sky. Like an impromptu firework, a bright white light explodes high above, expanding into colorful ribbons. Bobbie rushes up from the floor and over to the windowsill, leaning on the ledge to poke her head out for a better view. The night air smells electric as the hairs on her arms stand at attention.

In the distance, the horizon glows, iridescent and beautiful. Pinks and purples and blues paint the sky, as if the Northern Lights have lost their way and ended up over the weeds of Uncertain, Texas.

"Wow!"

Bobbie stomps into her slippers and rushes out of her room, down the hallway, past her mom in the kitchen, and out the front door.

"Bobbie Ann Broadbent! Where are you going? Bobbie Ann?" Her mother protests, pushing open the screen door as her daughter disappears into darkness.

Weeds slap against Bobbie's shins as she runs through the field toward the glowing horizon. Like a moth to a flame she is pulled without thought, toward the pulsating lights, having no control over where her feet take her as she bounds along the shores of Caddo Lake.

Vibrant colors dance atop the water, awash with energy, mirroring the dramatic performance in the sky, making Bobbie feel as if she is enclosed inside a mystical crystal ball. Nearing the spectacle, something pulls her focus—a sudden darkness, a shadow among the luminescence. She stops in her tracks. The silhouette of a man looms at the edge of the water, his back turned to Bobbie.

Spooked by the sudden realization she is alone in the dark and yards from home, she looks for a place to hide. She must conceal herself before the stranger notices her.

To her right, a patch of tall, dense Indian grass soars higher than her four-feet-nothing. It appears to say "Shhh…" as it sways in the breeze, beckoning her entrance, promising shelter, willing to keep her presence a secret. Bobbie quickly ducks into the grass and continues to tiptoe toward the dazzling light show and now, also, toward the stranger.

She wades through the stalks, gingerly parting them with her arms, inhaling their earthy aroma. Bobbie, ever so quietly, nears the stranger, being extra careful to pad lightly in her fuzzy slippers. He stands ashore, turned away from her, a lone braid knotted into the back of his long, jet hair. Something about that feels familiar. Backlit by the prismatic horizon, he raises his arms to the sky, as if to summon some grand and magical spell. Bobbie wonders if this phenomenon above is all his doing.

Brush smolders on the ground all around the man, an intentional circle of burning embers, making him the bullseye in a theoretical target. A breeze carries the smoke toward Bobbie, delivering it to her nostrils with a tickle, the fragrance unfamiliar to the child. It's certainly not a backyard campfire, built to singe the edges of a fluffy marshmallow skewered to a stick. It smells more like the funny cigarettes the big kids hide behind the barn to smoke. The ones that make them giggle. Bobbie pinches her nose—she can't sneeze now, it would surely blow her cover.

Bobbie sees the man has something in his hands, raised high to the heavens, something round, smooth and glowing. She takes a small step closer, peeking her face just far enough out of the grass to get a better look at the pretty object. Just one step closer and she'll have a clearer view. *Crack*! A brittle branch betrays her, rudely snapping under her foot, breaking the silence. She slaps her hand over her mouth to muffle her gasp, but it's too late now!

Frozen among the reeds, Bobbie pulls her arms tight to her sides and clenches her fists, not daring to move a muscle, willing herself invisible, trying to hold her quickened breath. Surely, if she stays still, he won't be able to see her.

The stranger spins around, spotting the tiny child

immediately, as her vibrant red hair glows under the luminous sky. *Oh no!* But Bobbie isn't afraid. Instead, she has an ache in her tummy, heavy with sadness. For the man's rich, ebony eyes are kind—familiar—as they grow wide with…recognition?

Bobbie can't believe her own, as the realization sets in. In a voice ever so small, she ekes, "Papa?"

"You shouldn't be here! Get back!" he says, pushing his hand toward her, and without him touching her at all, she feels a force as if he's shoved her. Bobbie stumbles back into the brush. It swallows her as she falls onto her bottom while the man, Maika Broadbent—her believed-to-be-dead father—pulled by some invisible bungee, disappears—into the ether.

Bobbie crawls back to the edge of the grass and peers out. She rubs her eyes, damp with melancholy, not believing what she's seen.

"Papa?" she whispers, confused, fatherless once again, scanning the grounds for his presence.

He is nowhere to be found. Bobbie slowly stands, wiping away familiar tears with the sleeves of her pajamas. Tears that blur her eyes, tears she's already cried for a father who has been gone for too many years. Surely this sighting was a figment of her imagination. She would think so if it weren't for the abandoned stone lying on the ground in the center of the glistening embers under a magical sky still flush with color.

Drawn by the orb, Bobbie moves closer to the edge of the lake, carefully stepping over the ring of smoldering leaves still billowing from the ground. She takes hold of the semiprecious stone, lifting it from the place her father once stood. The beautiful orb is about the size of a baseball and feels heavy in her small hands. It sparkles and still holds the warmth of her father—something she used to know. She closes her eyes, imagining his arms around her, keeping her safe. She shakes the image from her head. Surely, if her father was still around, he would come back to the family he loves. The stone no longer glows, but its energy makes her body tingle, and goosebumps flood her flesh.

But the warmth is short-lived. A chill runs through Bobbie and the hairs on the back of her neck stand at attention, as a feeling of dread washes over her. *Someone's here!*

It's not her father. Reflected in the lenses of her glasses, a luminous blue figure grows larger as it nears. Bobbie drops the stone and clamps her hands over her ears to stop the unbearable ringing as the ground rumbles under her feet. She feels as if she's floating, rising high above the earth—right before her world turns black.

BACK HOME

Bobbie ascends her front porch stairs, disheveled and dazed. Her body buzzes, as if a million bees have taken up residence inside her veins. Norma stands on the front porch, arms folded into herself, her mouth contorted into a shape only a disapproving mother could make.

"Where did you run off to young lady? And at this time of night?" Her stern expression can't hide the worry behind her soft, gray eyes. She pulls open the screen door and gestures with her arm, ushering her daughter into the kitchen.

"Sorry, Momma."

"What have you done to your glasses?"

"What?" Bobbie removes her glasses to get a better look at one shattered lens, splintered into a crystalline web.

"And your pajamas?"

Bobbie places her glasses back on and looks down at a kaleidoscope of herself. She unsuccessfully tries to brush the prickly burrs off her pajamas. She can feel the cool kitchen floor under one foot, free of its lost slipper.

"I...I don't remember. I must've fallen." She wasn't lying—she couldn't quite remember what pulled her out into the dark of night, nor what she encountered there.

"Never you mind, Bobbie Ann. Time for bed."

"Okay, Momma."

Step-flop, step-flop. Bobbie makes her way back to her bedroom, wearing one slipper, face crinkled in confusion, trying to remember just what it was that made her run out into the fields in the first place. *Step-flop, step-flop*. She remembered playing with her ants, watching their movements, and then…well, nothing. Bobbie enters her bedroom. Everything is the same as she left it—except for one important thing.

"Oh no!" she cries.

To her dismay, her ant farm has toppled over, its contents spilled everywhere. She rushes to the disaster, kicking off her other slipper. Sand is strewn about, it's even stuck between the threads of the braided rug on the old hardwood floor. The impressive network of tunnels, once meticulously preserved within the glass, now gone—destroyed, scattered about her floor.

Bobbie kneels on the floor, desperately trying to brush the mess back into the container. She gently moves the sand around to unearth her ants, hoping they haven't been injured.

"Wha—" Her eyes dart across the scattered grains. "Where are they?" With a heavy heart, she quickly, but carefully, distributes the sand, looking for her miniature friends. She couldn't find any. Not one tiny soul left for her to love.

"Oh no, oh no," she repeats, lifting the rug. No ants there. She scoots to her bed and peeks underneath—nothing but a few dusty board games and an abandoned sock. She frantically searches her room, looks into every nook and cranny, but cannot find one single ant. Not even a single file line trying to escape up the wall, over the sill, and out the open window.

The delicate sheers billow into Bobbie as she peers out the

window into the darkness, holding her empty, abandoned farm, wondering where in the world her ants have gone, and why in the world can't she remember?

HARRUMPH

Sunbeams burst through the bottom of a glorious cloud, in Godlike fashion, sending fingers of gold across Bobbie's face. In the history of beautiful things, this would be up there with one of the best, if someone would only notice. If only someone wasn't sulking on the front porch stairs, chin in her hands, trying not to look at the empty and abandoned ant farm sitting next to her. Bobbie wishes the cicadas would just stop humming—for today isn't a humming day. Today is a harrumph-ing day.

"Harrumph." She kicks the dirt with the tip of her sneaker, sending a little dust cloud up into the air. If the sky was going to insist on being beautiful, she'd make a tiny dirty cloud all her own, to match her mood.

Behind her, the screen door creaks, and she hears her mother's soft footfall. Norma sits on the step next to Bobbie and puts her arm around her daughter. Her mother smells of fresh baked bread and rose perfume.

"You still owe me an explanation of why you ran off last

night. You scared me." Bobbie picks at her shoelace as her patient mother continues. "There sure were a lot of shooting stars last night. Can't help but have 'em when the skies are as clear as they are. But you have just as good a view from this-here porch as you do out in that field—in the dark, where I can't see you."

"I know." Bobbie plays with the fanned end of her shoelace missing its aglet. "I'm sorry."

"It's okay. Next time, ask me to come along."

Bobbie thinks long and hard about why she didn't ask her mother to come along. If only she knew what drew her out into that field with such fervor. Even a good night's sleep couldn't help her remember.

Norma hugs Bobbie close. "What do you say you ride your bike down to McCreedy's and pick up a small bag of sand? You can treat yourself to an ice cream cone as well."

"Really?" Bobbie bubbles with excitement, and it's not about the ice cream, it's about the sand because she knows what's coming next.

"Yes. And when you get back, I'll help you round up more ants."

"Okay!" Bobbie pops up from the stair and gives her mom a peck on the cheek, decidedly leaving her grumpy mood behind. "Thank you, Momma!"

She runs off to her bike, propped on the old shed, and pushes it toward the dirt road.

"Be careful!" Norma calls out as Bobbie hops on and pedals off.

Bobbie's hair, an explosion of ginger corkscrews, billows behind her like a warning flag in the wind, alerting the local flora and fauna of her presence. She pedals along the crackling gravel, navigating the winding country road, like she's traveled so many times before.

The usual ride is to the five-and-dime, a little wooden house in the middle of town, the one that smells like mildew and cotton candy. It's there she'll wander about, her untied shoelace tick-ticking along the old creaky floor, as she'd peruse the countertops stocked with confections piled into big glass jars. She'll carefully select pieces of her favorite candies and drop them into a small paper bag, then bring them to Mrs. Perkins at the cast-iron register. Mrs. Perkins always wears a floral mumu that reminds her of her mom's good tablecloth. And she has a mole on her chin that reminds Bobbie of a wrinkly chocolate chip. But not the kind she'd ever want to eat. Bobbie will pay for the treats with the coins she earned from helping her mother with the household chores. She doesn't necessarily like sweeping the front porch or unclipping the clothes from the line. She'd much rather be farming for ants or nosing through her picture books. But once her dad disappeared, she knew she needed to help her mom around the house, for Bobbie was all she had. Well, her, and the ants. But her mother didn't really think of the ants as family, not the way Bobbie did.

As she rides toward town, she closes her eyes and inhales the local aroma of fresh cut grass and manure while passing the old barns and farmhouses along the way. A farmer rides on a rusty mower as a lazy cow lifts her head, slowly chewing, side to side, never missing a beat, as the streak of Bobbie whizzes by.

"Moo-cow!" Bobbie yells. The unfazed bovine returns to grazing, and Bobbie giggles at the cuteness.

Standing on her pedals, she coasts the bumpy road and reaches high to slap the old metal sign at the edge of town, the one that says "Welcome to Uncertain, Population 196." She knows life in Uncertain isn't actually uncertain at all. It's extremely predictable. For there are not many people, and everyone seems to do the same old thing, in the same old way, every day. Neighbors tend to their crops—planting, fertilizing, watering, and plowing—at the same times each day, during the same times each year. Down the road are a couple of cows and some goats who feed from the usual old trough. And it's likely you'll meet the same old souls camping and fishing on the banks of Caddo Lake. Her mother used to call it "small-town heaven." But not so much lately.

With a population of one hundred and ninety-six, everyone knows everyone, so folks are always watching out for each other. Sometimes, they are even a little too helpful. Like the time when Bobbie's father went missing. She remembers her mom not wanting "*one more damn casserole.*"

Because when her father disappeared, people showed up—with a parade of Pyrex, and sad exchanges…and lots of whispers. Bobbie kind of liked them—not the casseroles, because they tasted of mushrooms, nor the whispers, but the visitors. They filled the empty space her dad had left behind. Because, when her dad went missing, it left a hole in their family. Her mom stopped talking. She stopped eating too. She didn't seem to want any casseroles at all.

Bobbie floats through the memories in her head as she navigates the lazy turns.

On the opposite side of town, a farmer opens a creaking door to a vintage Ford pickup truck. One high-pitched whistle and his cattle dog hops onto the front seat. The farmer climbs in after and gives his happy pooch a scratch on the head.

One turn of the key and the truck whirrs awake, but not without a hiccup first. A shift into drive, and they make their way down a long, lazy path and onto the gravel road.

The farmer switches on the radio and an old John Denver song fills the cab, barely drowning out the squeaky seats.

"Thank God…I'm a 'sump'n, 'sump'n…" the farmer sings and drives. His dog gives him a sloppy kiss on the cheek, and the farmer hugs the pooch close with his free arm.

Bobbie exits McCreedy's General with a small bag of sand under one arm and an ice cream cone in her other hand. She licks the chilly confection as a few dairy cows moo in the background. There's nothing like sweet, creamy ice cream made fresh on the dairy farm. Nothing at all.

Bobbie drops the bag of sand into the basket fastened to the front handlebars of her bike and hops on the seat, pushing herself off to pedal back home, steering with her free hand.

Her handlebars wobble as she makes her way back along the gravely road. But soon, she gets the hang of steering with one hand while enjoying the quickly melting cone in the other. A dribble of vanilla drips from the cone to her wrist, and she leans in to give it a lick.

The old Ford truck maneuvers the curvy road, windows down, as the farmer now croons a howling rendition of "Luckenbach, Texas" by Waylon Jennings.

He steers the truck with one hand, and with the other, holds on to a raggedy dog toy. The other end of the toy is tightly clamped in the dog's mouth. The farmer pulls on the toy as the dog playfully growls at his owner during this traveling game of tug of war.

Bobbie lifts her head up to see an old blue pickup truck coming around the corner, in the opposite direction.

The farmer has a good grip on the dog's toy as he tugs and drives. He sees Bobbie pedaling toward him, in the opposite direction, on the other side of the road. The playful dog also sees Bobbie and barks, releasing the toy, which is still in the farmer's firm grip, propelling the farmer's arm hard to the left, causing him to steer the truck into Bobbie's lane.

Bobbie can barely hear the muffled horn over the shot of adrenaline coursing in her ears. In a flash, she sees herself at age seven, along with her father, as they play with her ant farm. Her father smiles at her. His kind eyes, once crinkled at the corners, unfold and turn wide with fear. In slow motion, he mouths, "Look out!"

The truck barrels toward Bobbie, blaring its horn.

BEEPS AND WHOOSHES

Vacuum pumps and EKG machines whoosh and beep, echoing in the small gray hospital room as they breathe life back into Bobbie. She lies unconscious in the bed, her small, broken body engulfed by casts and probed by tubes.

Norma tucks the waffle-knit blanket around the shape of her daughter, then sits in the chair next to the bed, worriedly wringing her own hands. She holds her breath as she eyes the doctor standing at the foot of Bobbie's bed, reading from his clipboard with the mundane enthusiasm of reviewing one's own shopping list.

"Seven broken ribs and a punctured lung," the doctor drones. "Cerebral hemorrhage, broken arm and foot, internal bleeding. It's a miracle this child survived."

"Praise be to God. I don't know what I'd do without her." Norma rocks back and forth on a static chair in an attempt to soothe herself. It's not working. "Is she gonna be okay?"

"Well, what we're looking for, is for her to wake up. To

recognize you. Then we'll know if we're on a good path to recovery."

"When can we expect that? For her to wake up?"

"No telling. Could be tonight, could be several days from now."

Norma clutches Bobbie's small hand, purple from the IV stuck into it. "She looks so small, so helpless. I should have never—"

"Accidents happen every day, Mrs. Broadbent, while people are doing the ordinary things they do. Now is not the time to blame yourself." The doctor squints at the pages on the clipboard. "If it makes you feel better, children heal very quickly. Much quicker than adults. So, let's keep positive thoughts on her progress, okay?"

Norma nods, wiping tears from her cheeks. She's unnerved by the dimple forming between the doctor's brows.

"However, she may take just a bit longer…considering…"

“Considering?”

“Considering her past surgeries.”

Norma gently lets go of Bobbie’s hand and sits a bit straighter. “Surgeries? She’s never had any surgeries before this. Hasn’t had as much as a tooth filled.”

“Hmmm…” The doctor flips through the pages on his chart, filled with multiple notations alongside X-rays of Bobbie’s broken body. He smiles sympathetically. Clearly the woman is in shock. “Okay, then, let’s keep an eye on your girl. I’ll be back in a bit.”

Norma brushes Bobbie’s hair away from her face as the doctor exits, leaving them bathed in the stressful cacophony of medical equipment.

Bobbie lays on what feels like a cold metal table looking up into glaring light as luminous blue bodies gather around her looking down at her. She can't make out any details. Only the outlines of those above her. She feels pinches and pokes but is paralyzed and can't move a muscle. She doesn't like this dream. She doesn't like it at all.

Norma pulls a few pages of the days gone by from the daily calendar that sits on the bureau in Bobbie's hospital room. She crumples them and tosses them into the trashcan. She's all but forgotten about the beeps and whooshes—can't even hear them anymore—as she smooths the sheets and blanket covering her daughter.

Norma rubs her own arms for warmth. The chilly air smells of medicine and field flowers. Handpicked bouquets, stuffed animals, and cards of well wishes, arranged on shelves, wait for Bobbie to awaken. None as impatiently as Norma, who is desperate to peer into her daughter's innocent eyes once again. She caresses Bobbie's face.

"My sweet baby. Momma's here." Norma swallows the lump attempting to strangle her words. She needs to be strong for her daughter. "Look at you, so strong. Doctor says you're beating all the odds. Healing up real nice. We're gonna be out of this-here hospital real soon." She scans the bruises on her daughter's broken body. Some have turned from a purpley-plum to a yellowish-green. "All these cuts and bruises. They'll be just a memory. You'll see."

Norma focuses on an odd wound below Bobbie's collarbone. She'd never noticed that one before. Different than her other injuries, it was pink and raised, like a keloid. Composed of a series of five graduating lines, from top to bottom, together they created the shape of a perfect triangle. Norma reaches out, and gently touches the wound, hopes it doesn't scar.

The beep of the EKG machine, counting the repetitive cadence of Bobbie's heartbeat, suddenly quickens. "Baby?" Norma says, startled. Bobbie doesn't move a muscle. Norma withdraws her hand from her child and holds it to her own chest. She thought she'd become accustomed to the machines. She attempts to soothe herself, inhaling for one…two…three…and lets her strained breath out slowly, but not without a small cough. She pulls her inhaler from her skirt pocket and takes in the medicine she regularly uses to calm her inflamed lungs.

Once again, she reaches for Bobbie, touches her triangular wound. Once again, the beeps on the EKG machine quicken. This time she keeps her hand on her daughter, and Bobbie's eyes flutter open.

Bobbie's world is dark and muffled as she drowns in the deepest depths of a pitch-black sea. Her chest feels heavy, her arms and legs pinned. She struggles to move, but her body won't obey her brain. If only she could open her heavy lids to see—to see just what it is that holds her captive in the dark.

She can't stop focusing on her thirst. *So thirsty.* Arid, like the desert, her throat is raw and sore.

Try harder! She concentrates on opening her eyes. A flutter, then two, then three. *Here we go!* Like the click of an old film projector, Bobbie's world emerges, frame by frame.

A figure begins to take shape against a blindingly bright background. She's seen it before. Luminous. Blue. A familiar rush of adrenaline rages through her veins like an ice-cold river. The figure leans in close. Then dissipates.

Bobbie's muted world becomes overwhelmingly loud and clear as white noise rushes into her ears, like raging rapids, carrying her back into the living. It's almost too much to bear.

Until a calming voice breaks through the noise.

“Oh! There you are, Baby.” Norma’s face slowly comes into view, calming Bobbie’s heart.

Norma scoops Bobbie up into a gentle embrace, and a warmth floods over Bobbie like a sedative, soothing her frigid veins. She can’t speak because there’s something in her throat, but she allows herself to close her teary eyes and bask in the safety of her mother.

Through the window, a flash illuminates the night sky.

SPILLED MILK

The flash of the camera compels Bobbie to rub the stars away from her eyes. “Ma-hum,” she protests, replacing her still-broken glasses, with her good arm.

“Sorry, Baby. We need a photo to document my strong girl finally back home. Four weeks is much too long to be at home without my baby girl.” Norma smiles ear to ear as Bobbie rolls her eyes up into her wild hair, looking adorably pathetic in her full-arm cast and walking boot. “Why don’t you go to your room and I’ll warm you some milk and bring it to you.”

“Can I stay up and draw a little?”

“Sure. You think you can manage?”

Bobbie shrugs, which lifts her arm, casted into a right angle, making it look like a petrified chicken wing, “I guess so,” she says as she hobbles off to her bedroom.

Bobbie colors at her desk in front of her open bedroom window, serenaded by an early evening symphony of weeping frogs and chirping crickets. The lace sheers, handed down from her great-grandmother, hang as heavy as the humid air, weighted with southern warmth. It's nights like this it's hard to sleep, unable to find relief from the hot Texas summers where the nights are just as hot as the days.

Bobbie thinks about her ants and the night her farm toppled, when her whole colony disappeared. She wondered why they just up and left her without a warning. Were they mad that she left them to chase the kaleidoscope in the sky? She wondered if her tiny friends were merely waiting for her to refill the structure with sand, and maybe they'd return, on their own, back to their bustling community. Back to her. She hoped they weren't lost, unable to find their way back. Or worse yet, maybe they found a new home and were happier there. Although, she wouldn't blame them. She did, after all, leave them for weeks as she recuperated in the hospital.

She stares at the photo on her desk, in the little gold thrift store frame. It's the one of her Dad and her, holding her ant farm. It was taken the day he gave it to her, for her seventh birthday. He'd made it with his own hands. She loved that day—they'd spent the whole afternoon filling it together. She missed those times, her dad. She missed her ants.

She didn't dare glance at the now-empty farm sitting on the end table, barren and void of life. It would only make her sad, and she was trying really hard not to cry. Her Papa used to say, *There's no use crying over spilled milk.* But she bet he'd have a different opinion over a spilled ant farm.

"Momma! I'm ready for my milk." She calls, adjusting herself in her seat, and placing the elbow of her casted arm onto her paper in an attempt to hold it still. She carefully outlines an ant with her good hand, trying to make it as anatomically correct as the rest of them. But this time, she uses a bright blue crayon instead of brown, and she takes her time coloring as best she can, in her unfortunate condition. A *crash* from the other room startles her, causing her to jerk her hand, sending a blue skid mark across the paper.

"Momma? What was that?" Bobbie listens, for her mother to answer. "Momma?"

Bobbie slides off her chair and hobbles out of her room as quickly as she can, heading down the hall and into the kitchen, where she finds her mother hunched over a chair gasping for breath. On the floor beneath Norma lies a shattered mug, a puddle of milk and a rescue inhaler.

"Momma!" Bobbie hobbles over to her mother, and picks up the inhaler, wet with milk. She's terrified by the panic in her mother's eyes.

"No…empty…" Norma gasps as she points to the cabinets across the room.

Bobbie stumbles to the drawers, opens the first and rifles

through with her good arm. Nothing. She looks back to her mom for guidance, but Norma is too weak as she kneels on the floor, fighting for breath. Bobbie frantically opens the second drawer, moving pencils and clothespins and batteries, and finds Norma's spare inhaler. She hobbles back to her mom and places the inhaler near Norma's mouth. Norma grasps it with both hands, squeezes, and inhales as best she can, coughing and wheezing like Bobbie has never seen before. Norma inhales another blast and lies on her back as her medicine works to calm her lungs.

"So…sorry…Baby…" she coughs.

Bobbie lies on the floor, close to her mother, draped over her as to melt into her, protecting her—eyes shut tight.

NIGHTMARES

Bobbie is lost in a field of wheat, soaring as high as the heavens. The stalks hiss loudly as the wind blows through, creating a violent white noise, making it hard for her to concentrate.

"Bobbie Ann..."

She hears her mother's faint voice in the distance and tries to make her way toward the sound, but the jelly-like substance under her bare feet suctions her to the ground.

"Momma?"

Bobbie strains to lift her legs, trudging through, parting reeds in a panic. It's useless. The minute she separates them, they surround her once again, encapsulating her within the cocoon.

"Bobbie Ann..." her mother whispers in the wind.

"Momma! Help me!"

The sticky liquid rises to Bobbie's calves as she turns left and right, searching for a way out, looking for any way to free herself. She is stuck in the thick liquid as it rises to her hips, then to her shoulders, then her neck. Panic sets in as she desperately tries to keep her head above the substance, craning her neck to inhale what's left of the air around her. It's no use: the jelly covers her mouth, fills her nostrils, covers her terrified eyes.

"Momma!" she screams, jolting up in Norma's bed, fiery curls stuck to her clammy forehead.

"Shhh…Baby. You've had a bad dream."

Bobbie scans the room, shaken from her nightmare, making sure she's safely back in her own environment. A clock on the bedside table flashes 3:00 A.M. She lies back down, scooting a little closer to her mother, curling up into her warmth, as Norma strokes her hair.

"There, there. Momma's here."

COLLECTING ANTS

The familiar crow of a rooster echoes in the distance as Bobbie lies in bed with her mother, watching the gentle rise and fall of Norma's chest, thankful she is breathing. Bobbie's focus changes from the pearlized buttons sewn to Norma's nightgown to the lazy dust particles floating in the sliver of light streaming through the bedroom window. Bobbie raises her hand and peeks through the space made between her thumb and pointer finger, as she pretends to squish the magical specks. The repetitive motion calms her busy mind.

"You up, Baby?" Norma says, her voice not yet awake.

"You scared me yesterday." Bobbie says, pressing her fingers together.

"I'm sorry, sweetheart." Norma gently grabs Bobbie's squishing hand and kisses it. "I didn't mean to cause you to have a nightmare. You wanna talk about it?" Bobbie shakes her head no. "What do you say we gather those ants today?"

Bobbie smiles and nods.

A group of turtles tilt their heads toward the sun, taking a peaceful respite from their adventures in swimming. They are unbothered by Bobbie and her mother as the duo walk, not too far from the shoreline.

Mother and child saunter beneath centuries-old cypress trees, romantically draped with Spanish moss. It's an otherworldly experience—the trees at Caddo Lake. Some line the shore, tall and strong, their branches outstretched and intertwined with each other, creating superhighways for the kamikaze squirrels. Others shoot straight out from the water, creating haunted forests in the lake, lining both sides of the waterway for boaters and fishermen to pass though. The trees are dreamy and eerie all at once, depending, of course, on the weather or the time of day. On a day like today, when the sky is blue and the butterflies flit, the moss-draped trees are as dreamy as they get as they gently filter and soften the sunbeams from above.

Norma carries Bobbie's ant farm, newly filled with sand and ready for its future inhabitants. Bobbie carries a small plastic bag filled with bread that's been buttered and sugared.

"Let's try here!" Bobbie says, excitedly, feeling the lightest she has in days. The idea of recreating her miniature world brings joy to her heart. *Today is a very good day!*

Norma sets the ant farm down on an old tree stump and unfurls a small blanket. Bobbie hands her mother the bag of sugared bread, and Norma removes a slice.

"Wait! Can I have one?" Bobbie asks, plopping herself onto the blanket, all smiles and giggles.

"Be careful, your arm is still not completely healed," her mother warns, as she hands Bobbie a slice of bread and joins her on the blanket. Norma removes another slice and tosses it on the ground. "Not gonna catch many ants if you gobble up their bait."

Bobbie giggles and eats her bread. They both stare at the ant farm, lovingly assembled by Bobbie's father. It's a simple, rectangular wooden frame supporting a piece of glass on either side, with a removable lid for easy access.

"Do you remember when your daddy made this for you?"

Norma asks.

"Yes…kind of." Bobbie's mind flashes back to the picture on her desk, reminding her not to forget her memories.

"After that, you'd spend the whole day together out here, collecting ants. Then you'd both come home and spend all night watching them work. It was precious. I couldn't help but be a bit jealous of the bond you shared."

Bobbie smiles at the memory, even if it is in bits and pieces from her young mind. "Momma? Why did Papa leave?"

"Don't know, Baby." Norma pauses at the thought, lost in the memory, replaying the moment that she's never come to understand. "He just up and disappeared one day. Didn't take nothin' with him…nothin' but our hearts." Norma fights back the glaze of tears that usually arrive at Maika's memory, trying to smile through it. Trying to be brave for her daughter. "That was three years ago. Can't dwell on the past, now, can we?"

Bobbie shrugs her shoulders: remnants of sugar crystals dot her pink lips, pursed together in thought. A faint memory of her father's face in the night, obscured by Indian grass, crosses her mind. "Momma, I think, maybe I saw…"

"Looks like we have a few takers," her mother excitedly interrupts.

A small group of ants mull around the sugar bread on the ground, exploring the sweet treat. But Bobbie notices something very important.

"No, not those, Momma!"

"Why not?"

"Look." Bobbie points to a large and familiar mound in the distance. Something an untrained eye would think a pile of sand. "Those are fire ants."

"Oh, right. Don't want any bites from those little buggers. Be itchin' for days." Norma blows at the ants and sends them scattering. "How can you tell them apart?"

"Practice, I guess." Bobbie studied her own ants for so long, she figured she'd probably recognize them if she came across them in the wild. "Oh!" Bobbie lifts her good arm from the ground to see a few "friendly" ants on her. "Here, Momma, these are good ones."

Norma removes the wooden lid, adorned with an acorn finial, from the farm, "Looks like you're sweeter than the sugar bread." She brushes the ants from Bobbie's hand into the container. The creatures willingly oblige, as they populate the environment Bobbie has made for them. She's already prepped it with food for her inhabitants.

Close by, a trail of ants heads toward Bobbie as if to have been summoned by her. Bobbie giggles as she helps her mother scoop them into the farm and close the lid.

Bobbie wedges the eraser end of a pencil underneath her cast, trying to scratch the itch that's making her cranky. It seems that after a successful day of ant hunting, everything in her body is on high alert. Her foot is puffy and throbbing and her the skin on her plaster-wrapped arm is irritated, and on top of it all, she can't keep her eyes open. She wondered if this is what her mother meant by plum-tuckered. Norma told her to be careful, to not push herself too hard, because her body was still healing, and if she did push herself, she'd be plum-tuckered out. Well, if plum-tuckered meant everything all at once, was fixing to make her scream—she sure was.

She fluffs the pillows on her bed and adjusts herself to get a good look at her ants. Surely that will take her mind off everything. She delights in the progress her colony has already made, building their thoroughfares within the panes of glass. She made sure to give them an extra teaspoon of sugar water so they would be fed and hydrated. She also made sure to have her mother help her carefully place the farm on the nightstand beside her bed so she could keep an eye on her tiny friends. This time, she was going to keep them safe and secure, with a watchful eye, every moment she got.

Bobbie runs her finger along the glass, tracing the trails, humming a little made-up melody. The ants seem to abandon their work and reverse their paths to follow her finger—a Pied Piper atop the glass.

"Huh?"

"Lights out, Bobbie Ann," Norma calls from the other room. "School tomorrow."

"Okay, Momma." Bobbie clicks off her light and lies down. But not before removing the flashlight from under her pillow. She clicks it on and points it at her farm. "Goodnight," she whispers, "don't let the bed bugs bite."

And, with a giggle, she's off to dream, knowing her friends are safe by her side.

SCHOOL

Bobbie unsuccessfully tries to straighten the barrette snapped into her chaotic hair as she stands in front of the mirror attached to her closet door. "Ugh," she grimaces at her reflection. It's the best job she can do with only one good arm.

Norma pops her head in the doorway. "Ready?"

"I don't want to go to school," Bobbie whines, closing her eyes and raising her face to the sky in despair—pouting the poutiest of pouts.

"What? My daughter, who loves learning? Who is the smartest in her class? Doesn't want to go to school?"

"They're going to make fun of me."

"Who is?"

"Crank Brady and his stupid friends. They always do."

"Bobbie Ann Broadbent, stupid is not a nice word. And since when have you cared what anyone else thought?"

"Look at me!" She presents herself to her mother with a huff.

For the first time, Norma gets a good look at her daughter

dressed for school. Her unruly hair is haphazardly pinned with mismatched barrettes and her clothing is cut to accommodate her full-arm cast and walking boot. She's adorably pathetic. Norma suppresses a giggle as she adjusts Bobbie's barrettes.

"Never you mind those urchins. You shine bright as the star you are." She gently pushes her daughter out by her shoulders to get another look at her. "You're interesting. What happened to you, is interesting. And, your friends are gonna want to know all about it." Norma pulls something from the pocket of her skirt. "Here! Maybe you can bring this pretty rock for show and tell."

Bobbie's eyes grow wide at the sight of the rock in Norma's hand. Like a bolt of lightning, her mind flashes back to a vision of her father holding the glowing stone up to a multicolored sky. A scene she'd forgotten until now.

"Where did you find this?"

"In the yard, when I was hanging clothes. Isn't it pretty?"

Bobbie nods her head, biting her bottom lip to prevent her

words from tumbling out. She didn't know how to tell her mother what she saw that night, even if it was coming back in bits and pieces. She didn't want to upset her mother with memories of her father. Especially when she, herself, didn't have a complete understanding of that evening.

"Come on," Norma says, kissing her daughter on the top of her head. "Let's get you off to school.

A bell rings in the classroom and the students rush to their desks, jockeying for their seats like a herd of cattle playing musical chairs. Bobbie hobbles in after the bell, past Mrs. Johnson who's busy writing out complex fractions on the blackboard. The room smells like rubber soles and adolescent sweat. The unseasonable hundred-degree heat from outside doesn't help as the the school's air conditioning struggles to cool the crowded classroom. "Whew, this weather is wild as a June bug on a string." Mrs. Johnson says to herself, as she fans herself with her print-out in between fractions.

Bobbie struggles as she looks for a desk, trying to manage her schoolbooks, her sack lunch, and her father's stone, all at the same time, awkwardly balancing them with her good and casted arm as she finds the seat near the back of the room that nobody wanted, the one with the wobbly desk. As she passes her classmates, she pretends to ignore the whispers. Out of the corner of her eye, she sees them, leaning over their desks, hands up to their mouths, gossiping into their neighbor's ear.

"Look at her."

"She's a cripple."

"Hobbly-Bobbly."

Bobbie plops her belongings onto her desk and sits, knowing full well her face is as red as it is hot. She pretends to adjust her books so she doesn't have to look up at anyone. Crank Brady, the redneck-iest kid in the school, and his friend Harley Jones turn in their seats, ready to mock the weakest link. They're dressed as if they'd both tripped and stumbled into a Goodwill clothesline on the way to school. Crank is twelve and much bigger than anyone else in class, yet his clothes are much smaller, allowing his potbelly to peek out of the bottom of his T-shirt. Crank apparently likes the fifth grade so much, he's on his third round. He and Harley chug chocolate milk out of glass bottles, like they're downing a couple of brewskis.

Crank lets out a loud, wet, burp. "What's with her hair? It looks like cats were suckin' on it."

The kids in the classroom hide their laughter from the

teacher, who is still busy at the blackboard, as they all stare at Bobbie. Harley—ever the follower—joins in on the insults, completing the offensive duo.

"Yeah, I thought she's an Injun. Injuns ain't got red hair."

"She's only half Injun."

"The shitty half!"

The boys laugh and snort at their own stupidity. Harley's on a roll now. "Carrottop-Half-Breed! Maybe her daddy is Howdy Doody." Harley laughs at his own joke, that no one else gets. They're all too young to understand.

"Who's Howdy Doody?" Crank is confused. "Wait. Is that, that *doll,* you have in your room? Damn, Harley, you're such a sissy!" The other kids laugh. No one is safe from Crank's vitriol, not even his best friend, Harley.

"It's a marionette. It was my grandfathers." Harley protests.

"A mari-a-what? Guess your grandfather was a sissy too!"

"That's enough, boys!" The teacher finally chimes in, peering over her readers. "Eyes forward. Take out your math workbooks."

The kids do as they're told, opening workbooks and wielding pencils fraught with bite marks and nubby erasers. Bobbie attempts to smooth her hair as she fights back tears. She hears a whisper from behind.

"I like your hair."

She turns around to see Noah Springfield seated behind her, leaning on his desk toward her. He has the warmest eyes she ever did see, and freckles tossed about his face as if God, Himself, was an abstract painter. One cluster appears to be in the shape of the Big Dipper. Bobbie gives Noah a shy smile. "Thanks, Noah." She leans her casted arm on his desk, for a respite from the weight of it all. It sure is exhausting, carrying that thing around all day. Her arm is wrapped from her palm to her shoulder, and there is a metal bar keeping it bent at a ninety-degree angle.

Noah notices the cast is an empty canvas. "Here, let me sign that." He pulls out two markers, a red one and a black one from the backpack tucked under his desk. He signs his name on her cast with the black one and draws a little red rowboat with the other. Bobbie smiles.

"Ahem." The teacher taps her foot, until all eyes are forward. Bobbie turns around in her seat, blushing, and the teacher gives her a wink and a nod. She's always been Mrs. Johnson's favorite. Maybe that's why the other kids tease her. "Okay, class," Mrs. Johnson begins, "this is the kind of math you'll be learning next year, in the sixth grade. So, I want you to get used to looking at the problems now, and they won't be so intimidating later. Next year, you'll learn how to multiply and divide fractions." The students groan in unison. "Does anyone want to attempt to solve the first problem along with me?"

A sea of blank faces stares back at the teacher. Bobbie looks around and slowly raises her good hand. Mrs. Johnson points with her piece of chalk. "Bobbie Ann?"

"Sss-sixty five and three quarters?"

The teacher nods and does a quick workout on the board. "Correct! What about the next one?" Mrs. Johnson scans the room, but no one dares make eye contact. They're all busy scribbling and erasing and scribbling once again in their notebooks. "Anyone have an answer? No?" She sees Bobbie Ann's hand in the air. "Okay, Bobbie Ann?"

"Seventy-two over one-fifty."

The teacher works it out on the board, and arrives at the same answer. "Correct, again." Mrs. Johnson casually walks the aisles, glancing at everyone's work, making sure they have copied her lead from the blackboard. She notices Bobbie Ann's workbook is blank, as if she's doing the math in her head. She also notices Crank and Harley not paying any attention. "Boys, no drinks in class." They both chug their milk, dry. "Next problem. Anyone else want to try?" Silence and scribbling. "Anyone?"

The class is too quiet for Bobbie Ann's comfort. It's like

the pause in a scary movie before the hideous creature pops out of the darkness. She reflexively breaks the silence. "Thirty-nine point five. Sixty-two and three quarters, and one hundred and seventeen. Those are the last three."

Mrs. Johnson, flustered, looks at the board, then at Bobbie Ann and her blank workbook. "How did you—?"

"*Buuurrrp*!" Crank interrupts the teacher, and the students explode into laughter. Crank stands to bow, relishing the attention. Mrs. Johnson is not having it.

"Crank Brady! In your seat! Now!"

He obeys, then turns back to stare at Bobbie. "Wow! You really are a freak!"

Harley chimes in, "Yeah! Half-breed, whole freak!"

"Boys!" Mrs. Johnson yells.

No one pays attention to Mrs. Johnson. The class becomes unruly, like a cage full of wild chimpanzees, hooting and hollering. They all laugh and stare—all but Noah, who sits quietly at his desk—pity written all over his whimsically-freckled face. Bobbie doesn't know what's worse, the jeers or the pity. Harley points at Bobbie and laughs. The whole scene plays out in slow motion. Bobbie's had enough. She rises from her desk, anxious and trembling with anger, gripping her father's moonstone with her good hand, her casted hand on top. She glares at Harley, fighting the urge to throw the heavy orb at him. She squeezes it harder, as overwhelming emotion threatens to rip through her flesh.

Suddenly, the stone begins to glow, luminous and pulsing, quieting the crowd. Bobbie doesn't notice the light. Her focus is on Harley, whose face turns serious as his stomach loudly gurgles. Bobbie continues to stare him down, furiously shaking, not knowing what's come over her. Her palms vibrate as the stone glows brightly. Tingles travel up her arms. Harley's eyes begin to water, and his cheeks fill with air as panic knits his brow. He violently vomits his chocolate milk, a sour projectile across the classroom. The kids scream in horror as they run from the mess.

Mrs. Johnson runs to Harley in a fluster. "Oh my gosh! Kids, make yourselves busy while I take Harley to the nurse. Noah, you be hall monitor." Noah hops up from his desk to take his position in the hall as the teacher escorts a crying Harley toward the door, calling out one last instruction. "Kids, be nice to Bobbie Ann. Maybe sign her cast?"

Everyone is huddled away from the puddle of putrid milk, just staring at Bobbie. The crowd is silent. Crank studies Bobbie's stone from afar, now back to its original, milky color. Maybe he just imagined it. He shifts his eyes to her cast and a sideways smirk contorts his face. He whispers to his classmates. They whisper to each other, nodding in agreement.

"Uh, sorry, Bobbie Ann. Harley's an idiot," he says, fixing his face to look somewhat innocent. "We'll sign your cast. Can we? Sign your cast?"

Bobbie hesitates, looking down at her cast adorned with Noah's little red boat. Everything inside her says no, but it would be nice to have more signatures and artwork to decorate such a boring thing. And maybe if she lets people sign it, they will be nicer to her. *What's happened to you is interesting. Your friends are gonna want to know all about it.* Her mother's words fill her head. Bobbie slowly nods yes, placing her fully casted arm—a perfect right angle, atop the desk.

"Great!" Crank is eager. "I'm first!" He grabs a marker out of someone's hand. "Close your eyes, it will be a fun surprise."

Bobbie closes her eyes. She can feel the drag of the markers as her classmates take turns signing her cast. One by one, they add their own personal marks. A small smile grows on her face, maybe her mother was right, she is hopeful she will now be accepted into the community.

"Oh! One more for me!" Crank says. Bobbie feels a bit of a scribble. "There, done!"

Bobbie opens her eyes to her smirking classmates. Once again, they burst into laughter. Bobbie looks down at her cast. It takes a minute—for it to register—all the horrible things scribbled on to the permanent plaster wrapped around her arm. *Half-breed, Freak, Brainiac-Maniac, Carrottop.* Awful words, written in big letters by the people now laughing at her. Even Noah's signature and pretty red rowboat are scribbled over.

"Aargh!" Bobbie screams. She hobble-runs out of the classroom, past Noah in the hallway, past Mrs. Johnson exiting the nurse's office, out the door of the school and down the stairs. She clomps faster and faster, her injured foot tender from all the thunking. She clumsily stumbles over herself and skids across the ground, onto her face—skinning her knee along the way. She rolls over into the grass on the side of the path, sobbing, burying her face deep into the sod, hating every minute of today. She knew it was going to be a horrible day. She tried to tell her mother, but her mother wouldn't listen. Bobbie rolls onto her back and looks at the sky, knee burning, as tears fall away from her eyes and pool in her ears.

"Daddy, why did you leave us?" She cries to the heavens, knowing no one will answer. She stares up at the clouds, blurred with tears…or is it something else that distorts her view? She wipes her eyes to get a better look. A transparent orb hovers over her face. Silent. She blinks to make sure she's not hallucinating. Is it her guardian angel come to help her? A fairy godmother? It disappears as fast as it came. She blinks again, frozen, wondering what to do next. Her bruised knee throbs to its own beat while the broken heart in her chest races.

Why do they have to call her half-breed? Of all the horrible things, she hates that the most. Like she isn't a full person? Which half would they accept? Her Native American Dad's or her white-bred West Texas Mother's? Yes, she is an anomaly, with her shock of thick, coiled red hair and blue eyes and her tawny freckled skin. But she is a whole person, just like everybody else.

The earth feels hot under her, but somehow its warmth softens her anxiety, releasing the tension in her small broken body. That, and the tickle on her hand. She raises her hand to her face to see a lone ant has hitched a ride. She watches the ant travel in between her fingers. In and out it treks, from behind to the front. It soothes her—the ant's journey. Like a meditation, it calms her nerves. She sits up and takes a breath. *What's this?*

A trail of ants has formed a single file line, and have crawled up her wounded leg and onto her skinned knee. Intuitively, they encircle her brush-burn, like Native Americans ritualistically dancing around a campfire. Round and round they close in, over the brush-burn, until they cover it—the whole wound, until she can't see it any longer. Round and round they expand, exposing the space, and once again, travel single file, down her leg and into the grass.

Bobbie stares at her knee—once skinned and bleeding, her brush-burn now healed. Only fresh, pink, skin remains.

Norma swings open the screen door, and Bobbie falls into her mother's embrace, clutching onto the safety of home.

"I'm so sorry, Baby." Norma kisses the top of her daughter's head. "Mrs. Johnson called to tell me what happened. She's worried about you. Says you can do your lessons from home until you feel better. Says you're way ahead of those other brats anyway."

Bobbie didn't want to tell her mother *I told you so,* it didn't really matter anyhow. She was just happy to be back home, back to her mother, back to her ants—the community that always accepted her just as she was.

MOONSTONE

A lone paper flier blows in the wind and catches on the old wooden siding of the local Optician's office in downtown Uncertain. On the paper, the faded printing of a missing person's notice, dated 1993—the face, Maika Broadbent, Bobbie's father. The paper blows away just as Bobbie and her mother exit the office, Bobbie's glasses repaired. Her walking boot is gone and she has a smaller cast on her arm; this one stops before her elbow and doesn't carry the taunting of her classmates. Her newly exposed bicep looks thin and frail, but the doctor assured her it would be back to normal in no time. She couldn't wait: she didn't want to look like a praying mantis on top of everything else. The weeks at home had been good for Bobbie—her body healed quickly. Unfortunately, her spirit still needed some time.

Mother and child walk through a bustling farmer's market in town, where colorful signs announce a festival—an honorary celebration of the Caddo Nation. Bobbie remembers the lessons in school teaching the kids about the Caddoans and how they were forced to leave their homes along the Red River in

Louisiana after the Louisiana Purchase. They even had a little play, acting out how they emigrated from Louisiana to other areas, with some settling in Texas. However, Bobbie already knew this, as her father always told her stories about his local ancestors and how only a few remained.

"Most Caddo left Texas," he would say. "But those who did choose to stay took up residence, right here, in Uncertain. Caddo Lake is, after all, named after the Caddoans."

Bobbie's father taught her to be proud of her dual heritage. "We are all connected," he would say, "every Nation across the United States. We are all family."

Today, the remaining Nation were integrated within the farmers' market, selling their wares. Bobbie and Norma passed tables creatively staged with pottery, piled with jewelry and woven baskets and blankets. It brought interest and excitement to otherwise unremarkable Uncertain.

Norma, more concerned about stocking her pantry, places vegetables into a tote while Bobbie wanders the other vendors, eyes big as saucers. She is drawn to a table where a Caddo elder sells jewelry, handcrafted of sterling silver and semiprecious stones, mined from the earth.

"Oh! Pretty!" Bobbie squeals, noticing a ring. Its decorative stone is much like that of her father's magical one. The rounded orb is set in a braided silver bezel, on a silver band, etched with tiny stars.

"Moonstone," says the elder, picking up the ring and handing it to Bobbie.

"It's magical," Bobbie says as she holds it up, inspecting its luminescence.

"As are you, little one."

"Is it from the moon?" she asks, excitedly.

"From Mother Earth," says the gentle elder, the wisdom of the world in her old eyes, "empowered by Father Moon."

Bobbie holds the ring in reverence. The stone is soft white, iridescent, and embedded with an opalescent rainbow that disappears and reappears as Bobbie turns the ring. "Wow!"

"In darkness, when Father Moon is full, you can harvest the energy of the Great Spirit in the sky. But only if you're pure of heart, and only if you believe."

Bobbie calls to her mother, who is inspecting lettuce nearby. "Momma, look at this!"

Norma joins her daughter and smiles at the elder, whose long white hair is just as wild and curly as Bobbie's. She sees the ring in her daughter's hands. "It's beautiful."

"Can we buy it?"

"I'm sorry, Baby, we can't. Not this month. We just had your glasses repaired…and the hospital bills."

Bobbie is disappointed, but understands. She holds the ring out toward the elder, but the elder holds up a hand, wrinkled by a lifetime of experiences. "No, you keep it."

Norma lowers her voice. "I'm so sorry, we can't pay you for—"

"My gift," the elder insists. "This belongs to her, was meant for her. She's been touched by the stars."

“I don’t understand,” Norma says, confused.

“She has the mark.”

“Can I, Mom?” Bobbie, interrupts.

Norma sees a glimmer in her daughter’s eyes, one that was previously extinguished by her elementary bullies. She is desperate for her daughter to be happy and would purchase the ring if she had the means. The elder nods at Norma, and something in her heart says okay, as she sets her pride aside and accepts the offering. She nods at Bobbie.

“Eek!” Bobbie excitedly slides the too-big ring onto her pointer finger, and the weight of the stone spins it around, pointing it toward the ground. She smiles a big cheesy smile at her mother, “I’ll grow into it!”

Norma chuckles, smiles warmly at the elder, and mouths *thank you*, then reminds Bobbie of her manners. “What do you say?”

Bobbie grins at the elder. “Thank you so much!”

“Believe in yourself, Little Moonstone. Use your

knowledge to heal this world."

Norma nods at the elder, and she and Bobbie continue on their way. Bobbie admires her new ring, squeezing her fingers together to prevent it from turning. "Momma? What did she mean, I have the mark?"

"I'm not sure, Baby," Norma says as she takes her daughter's hand. "Would you like some lemonade?"

"Yes, please!" Bobbie says, holding her mother's hand to her cheek. "Today was a very good day."

A diffused golden glow kisses the lake, gilding the ripples, as Norma pulls her old car up into the driveway. Bobbie leans against the passenger window, exhausted after a long day in town, eyes closed, mouth open, *catching flies* as her dad used to say. She's had a heck of an adventure for a healing ten-year-old. The car's tires crackle over gravel, shooing the neighborhood chickens away, just barely enough not to hit the lazy birds.

"What's this?" Norma says.

Bobbie opens her eyes to see a familiar truck parked in the driveway. The tall and slender man standing next to it appears to have "cleaned up" after a long day in the field, wearing what must have been his best jeans, a faded, crisp crease worn into the front of the legs after years of ironing. His playful dog sweeps the ground with his tail, tip-tapping his front paws, as he barely but obediently sits next to the old farmer.

Bobbie and Norma exit their car and walk toward the duo. The man removes his well-worn cowboy hat, with a hand tan and leathered from hard farming in the hot Texas sun.

"Howdy, Missus."

"Hello." Norma and Bobbie say in unison. The farmer's dog pops up and runs to Bobbie, who welcomes him with open arms. The happy pooch shakes his whole bottom in excitement.

The farmer addresses Bobbie "Lil' Missus, c'ain't feel but awful 'bout what happened to 'ya, on a count-a us."

Bobbie looks down and bashfully kicks pebbles, then pushes up her new glasses. "It's okay, it was an accident." The dog jumps up trying to lick her face, and the farmer lets out a quick whistle, heeling the dog at Bobbie's feet. She giggles.

"It's not okay." Norma adds in her most stern, mother-voice. "Certain persons need to be paying attention when they're driving."

"Yes ma'am. Been beatin' ourselves up about it. Wanted to make it right."

Bobbie scratches the scruff on the back of the dog's neck; the pooch's tongue unfurls in a happy grin. The farmer approaches his truck and opens the squeaky tailgate. He pulls a red bicycle from the back bed and wheels it over to Bobbie.

"Wanted you to have this. Ain't much, but wanted to make amends, somehow."

Bobbie's eyes light up at the site of the two-wheeler with hand-sewn leather seat and matching tassels hanging from the handlebars. "Oh, wow! This might be the best day ever! " Bobbie looks to her mom for approval. Norma nods. "Thank you!" Bobbie tells the farmer without being reminded. She runs to grip the bike handles, and the dog follows, just as excited as her.

"That's mighty kind of you, sir." Norma can tell the previously owned bike had been refurbished, most likely by the farmer's own hands—a man, who she presumed, couldn't afford many extras. She is thankful for the gesture.

"Anything y'all need, you just let me know. Okay? I'm real close. Down at ol' Itchy Acres."

Bobbie giggles. "Where?"

"Down at the ol' Johnson farm. Call it Itchy Acres on a count-a all those gosh-durned fire ants…pardon my French.

Mounds upon mounds of ants be livin' in that-there ground! Should charge admission for all the lookey-loos. Trespass 'bout ev'ry other day to come see 'em. Mounds as tall as ol' Clarence here," he says, gesturing at the happy pooch. "If y'all wanna stop by, I got a bell fer yer bike. Forgot to bring it with me."

"Can I come to see the ants?"

"Long as yer momma says it's okay."

Norma places her hands on her daughter's shoulders. "Yes, but another time. We've done enough for one day."

The old man nods, puts his hat back on, and opens the door to his truck. One whistle, and Clarence hops in, a happy passenger looking forward to his next journey. The farmer climbs in and closes the creaky door. He touches the brim of his hat and winks at Bobbie. "Name's McElroy. I'll be lookin' fer ya."

CONSTELLATIONS

The spangled night sky over Uncertain is generous, presenting to Bobbie a continuous light show of stars, both static and shooting. She lies on a blanket in her front yard, illuminated by the full moon, her ant farm carefully placed close to her, steadied on a smooth, flat piece of slate. She can see her mother puttering in the kitchen through the soft warm glow of the window. Most importantly, Norma can see her daughter as well.

A soft breeze carries a mixed bouquet of mint and basil planted in the raised garden bed, not too far from Bobbie, as she points out the constellations in the clear, night sky.

"Big Dipper…Little Dipper…Orion…" she whispers, among an orchestra of crickets. She's studied all the galactic formations in the picture books in her room at least a hundred times, and she has them all memorized down to every last star visible to the human eye.

She admires her new ring, sitting lopsided on her hand, as she moves her finger along the stars in Orion's belt. She counts aloud, "One, two, three…four?" She counts again. "One, two, three…four!" She sits up quickly, and clicks on the flashlight by her side, curious at her finding. She thumbs through her book of stars until she finds Orion's page, until she finds her confirmation in black and white.

Bobbie has studied the stars long enough to know Orion's belt only ever has three stars. And her book confirms it. But tonight, another star seems to have inserted itself into the mix. Bobbie places her book and flashlight aside and sits criss-cross-apple-sauce, staring up at her new finding. She puts her thumb and pointer finger close together and pretends to pinch the star between them, pretends to hold on to it, squinting her eyes to get a better look.

"Look, guys", she says to her ants, "can you see it?" Then, "Where did you come from?" she says to the star.

The heavenly body glows brighter, bigger, and bluer than the others. And, surprisingly, so does the stone in her ring! Together, with the star, it glows softly, emitting a halo of light, all on its own.

Quick as lightning, she has a vision of her father holding his glowing stone up to the heavens. *Moonstone!*

"Bobbie Ann! Time to come inside!" her mother calls.

Startled, Bobbie pulls her hand back. "Coming!"

NOAH

Noah bounds up the stairs to Bobbie's front porch, scooping up the newspaper that's been thrown on the doorstep. He doesn't bother to notice the headline, *Cosmos Shifting In Orion Constellation*, as he knocks on the screen door.

Norma opens the door with a friendly smile. "Hi, Noah."

"Hi, Mrs. Broadbent," he says, jeans rolled into a high-water cuff. "Here's your paper, and Bobbie's schoolwork for the week."

"Why, thank you, Noah." Norma chuckles at the unruly cowlick drawing attention to itself at the crown of Noah's head. She can tell the boy worked hard on wetting it down, trying—unsuccessfully—to keep it tamed as it blows in the breeze.

Noah digs into the front pocket of his baggy jeans. "Oh… and she left her rock." He presents the moonstone to Norma, who takes it from his open palm.

"Thank you, Noah, that's very sweet of you."

Bobbie emerges from behind her mother, and Noah's face lights up. "Hi, Bobbie. Can you come out and play?"

Bobbie looks up at her mom. “Can I, Momma?”

Before Norma can get the words, *of course*, out, Bobbie and Noah run off. “But not for too long!” She calls out. “Best to keep up on your schoolwork! You are not on vacation, young lady!”

“Okayyyy…” Bobbie sings, her voice trailing off as she skips away.

As Norma walks back into the house she looks down at the stone in her hand. Hearing Bobbie’s giggles in the distance, she grips it with a smile.

Bobbie and Noah walk the banks of Caddo Lake, skipping stones across the water along the way. A red-shouldered hawk follows behind, flying from tree to tree, as the two enjoy a lazy, hazy, Texas afternoon. Noah forages for flexible twigs, pulling and bending them as he goes, tossing the snappy ones aside, and keeping the rubbery ones, while Bobbie blows wishes from dandelions—hoping for more days just like this.

During a quick respite, the two friends sit along the silty shore, listening to the water lap a rhythmic tune, both of their shoes tossed aside.

"What's that?" Bobbie asks as Noah weaves his found twigs together into a little vessel.

"A boat."

"It's not gonna float. Not with all those holes."

Noah chuckles and hands it to her. "I know." He looks off to the lake, wistfully. "I'm building my own boat with my uncle. A real boat."

"A big boat?" Bobbie inspects Noah's handiwork.

"No, a rowboat. I'm going to paint her red and name her Noah's Ark."

Bobbie thinks back to the little red boat Noah drew on her cast, and smiles. "That's not very original…the name, I mean." She hands the plaited twigs back to Noah.

They laugh, and Bobbie lies back, eyeing the clouds above that signal the impending storm slowly rolling in. Noah pulls grass from the ground and tosses it up, into the growing breeze. He lies back to join Bobbie in contemplating the clouds. Some are heavy with rain, dark in the belly—like something is hiding inside.

"Noah, do you believe in aliens?"

He hesitates to answer. "I don't know." Of course he does —every ten-year-old boy believes in aliens. But maybe this is a trick question. "Why do you wanna know?"

Bobbie shrugs. Maybe she shouldn't talk about these things. She doesn't want her only friend to think she's weird. The red-shouldered hawk flies over, a shadow across them both, and makes his way to the shelter of his nest, high up in a cypress tree.

"Is that bird following us?" she asks.

"I think so," Noah says. "Or me, at least. They always do."

"What?"

"Yeah. Kinda weird, isn't it?"

"I don't know, I think it's kind of cool."

"Me too." They lay silent for a moment. Then Noah says, "I wish I could fly."

"Where would you fly to?"

"I'd fly farther than the moon."

Bobbie turns her head to look at Noah. "Oh, I thought you meant with wings. You'd need a rocket ship for that."

"Yeah." A drop of rain hits Noah on the forehead, and he wipes it off. "Maybe after I build my boat, I'll build a rocket ship." He holds his handmade boat and tilts it upward, imitating a liftoff, then flies it around in his hand. The two watch Noah's ark of twigs peacefully hover on by.

Thunder *booms* out of nowhere, and they both jump to their frightened feet. The clouds burst, sending huge droplets to earth, soaking the friends as they scoop up their shoes and run off screaming and laughing, signaling the perfect end to a perfect day.

CRANK

Farmer McElroy waves goodbye, and Bobbie rings her new bell, pushing her bike carefully, as she snakes it through the multiple fire ant mounds at Itchy Acres. The old man sure was right, he should charge admission for people to come to witness the spectacle. Bobbie'd never seen so many ant mounds in all her life. And they were big, bigger than any she'd ever imagined. She was extra careful not to disturb them because if she did, she knew those fire ants would come out fighting. She knew they would attack her, and bite her, and those bites hurt—a lot. And not just when they bit you, but also after, when you swell up and turn all oozy and itch like crazy, and you scratch so hard your skin comes off.

She's so glad she didn't collect fire ants. Her ants were calm and kind. She admired them now, looking at the glass farm, nestled in the basket of her bike. She didn't tell her mom she was going to take it with her to Itchy Acres because she knew her mom would say no. But Bobbie really wanted Farmer McElroy to see it, since he was such a fan of ants.

"Well-now," he'd said when she showed him the thing closest to her heart. "That-there is some kinda habitat you got goin'. 'Bout a thousand pets in there. I just got, ol' Clarence, here. He's all the pet I need."

Clarence didn't look up from his lazy nap on the front porch, he just rolled over, with a yawn and a big stretch, exposing his belly to the sunshine.

Now, as she pushes her bike along, Bobbie wonders why the farmer didn't think of his cows and pigs and chickens as pets. Maybe she'd have more pets when she grew up. She knew she couldn't have any right now, not with her mom's asthma the way it was. Maybe, when she grew up, she'd have a whole farm. Well, after she became a scientist first. She wondered if scientists had farms.

"Where ya going, freak?"

A chill up her spine, Bobbie's flesh erupts in goosebumps at the sound of Crank's all-too-familiar voice. She looks behind to see him riding his bike toward her, his calamitous energy buzzing forward. She pushes her bike a little faster.

“Leave me alone, Crank!”

Crank speeds up, pedals around her, and skids to a stop in front of her. He throws his bike to the ground and sticks his nose in her basket.

“What’s that, in there?”

“Nothing.” Bobbie tries to steer around him, but Crank blocks her, and manhandles her ant farm from the basket.

“Hey! Don’t touch that!” Bobbie’s bike falls to the ground, thunking right next to a mound, disturbing a flurry of ants who rush to the surface.

“Why, freak? What is it?”

“Give it back!” Bobbie doesn’t tell him what it is. She desperately tries to reach it, but the older boy is so much taller than her, and he has it raised high in the air.

Crank pushes her away to get a better look at her farm. “Huh?” He sees the ants traveling along their tunnels, minding their own business. “Ew! Bugs!” Crank throws the farm to the ground and stomps on it.

"No! Stop!" Bobbie screams.

Crank continues to stomp on the ground, disturbing the mounds around him, and fire ants begin to emerge from deep within the earth. Crank continues to taunt Bobbie, picks up the broken structure, and hurls it into the lake.

"Crank, no!" Bobbie wails, running toward the lake, as she watches her precious ant farm quickly sink. "Nooo," she cries, her face in her hands, trying to catch her breath in between heart-wrenching sobs.

"Aw…Crybaby cry! I killed your bugs. You really are a freak!"

Rage bubbles up inside Bobbie's slight frame, mirroring the bubbles emerging from the water above her sinking ant farm. It's nothing she's ever felt before, this hatred, as it fills her with the strength of a thousand men. She turns and runs toward the taunting bully and shoves him down to the ground. Hard. Crank lands on top of the biggest fire ant mound of all.

Immediately, ants swarm all over Crank as he rolls on the ground, wailing. They cover his hands, feet, and face; they scatter underneath his clothing, in his hair and his ears, and they bite him—a thousand pinches all at once, synchronized and purposeful. Crank jumps up screaming, trying to brush the ants off as he runs away crying, howling in pain.

Bobbie looks at the lake. Her broken farm, heavy with sand, sank quickly, disappearing into the dark water.

HEALING

Bobbie rubs her thin, scaly wrist as her legs dangle from the examination table in the small medical room. She can't believe how much an arm can shrink, being in a cast for all those weeks. She holds it up to show her mother, who gives her an empathetic smile from the chair beside her.

The doctor rolls over to them on his stool. "Whelp, that's the end of it. Good as new."

"It's so small," Bobbie says, still devastated about yesterday's encounter with Crank.

"Yep. But it will be back to normal in no time. Just like your bicep." Bobbie looks at her whole arm, the darn thing looks like one of the sticks Noah uses to weave his creations. The doctor hands Norma a small plastic bag. "This contains some exercise instructions for her to build her muscle back up. And some lotion for the dry skin."

"Okay, thank you, Doctor."

"You're good to go," he says, as he wheels over to the door, and pops it open. He pulls a swirly lollipop out of his lab coat pocket and hands it to Bobbie with a wink. Bobbie likes the doctor, whose eyes are enlarged by his spectacles, just like hers. She gives a half smile. It's all she can muster in her current state. Bobbie and Norma head through door, and into the waiting room on their way out.

"Crank Brady," a receptionist calls, from behind a little porthole, cut into glass, in the front of the office. Bobbie stiffens at the name. "The doctor will see you now."

Bobbie scans the waiting room to see Crank and his mother rise from their seats. Crank's face is swollen and speckled with oozing ant bites. He scratches his equally bitten arms and body, looking absolutely miserable. On his way into the examination room, he sees Bobbie but averts his eyes.

Was that a glimmer of fear? As Crank passes Bobbie, she whispers, "Freak."

Bobbie inhales the sweet smell of wisteria twisted around the gazebo in the middle of town as she stands on the stairs, impatiently waiting for her mother to take the photo. People pass by, smiling at the site of the cute girl with wild hair. She doesn't notice.

"Momma," she whines.

"Just one second, Lil' Bit. I need to document this moment."

"I just got my cast off. I didn't win any awards."

"I know, Baby, but you're all healed. Praise Jesus. Say cheese."

"Cheeeesus." The additional eye roll is certain to make a great memory.

"Bobbie Ann Broadbent!"

Bobbie giggles, and her mother snaps the photo. It's the best she's gonna get.

"Ahhh…Little Moonstone," a familiar voice calls.

Bobbie runs off the stairs, happy to have a reason to quit

the photo shoot, and greets the elder, who is carrying a small basket of interesting supplies.

"Look! I'm wearing my ring!"

"I see." The elder hovers her hand over Bobbie's newly freed arm. "All healed now." Bobbie nods. The elder looks to Norma. "She's Caddo?"

Norma nods. "Half. Her daddy."

The elder hovers her hand in front of Bobbie's triangular scar of five graduating lines on her collarbone, the only remnant left of her accident. Contrary to Norma's wishes, it never seemed to heal. Bobbie instinctively reaches to touch it.

"Your power is strong, Little Moonstone. Intelligence beyond the clouds. But, I sense sadness," the intuitive elder states as Bobbie hangs her head. "You lost something important to you. Someone took it from you."

Bobbie nods, looking up at the elder with pathetic eyes saved mostly for cartoon characters. The elder hands the small basket to Norma and pulls a bundle of sage, a lighter, and a hawk quill from it. She lights the sage until the edges are afire, then blows it out, waiting for the little red embers to die down, waiting for the bunch to smolder. She then wafts the smoke around Bobbie using the feather. Bobbie recognizes the smell. Her memory flashes back to the burning ring on the ground around her father the night she ran off to witness the multicolored sky.

"You will build it back. Bigger. Better. It will come back to you again." The elder hands Bobbie the quill. "But not until the great sky hunter brings a message from the heavens. Be patient, Little Moonstone—it won't come back to you for many seasons." The elder turns to Norma. "She will be fine In'a. You've done your job. You've taught her well."

"Thank you," Norma says, suddenly filled with melancholia. "We'd best be going now." She gently ushers Bobbie away. Bobbie looks back at the elder, who smiles and nods, filling Bobbie's heart with the familiarity of family.

NIGHTMARES

Bobbie pushes through dense wheat, jelly-like liquid under her feet, accompanied by a low-rolling fog. Just beyond, a blue glowing light shines between the reeds. She parts the wheat to see her father, standing with his back to her, his magical moonstone raised high to the sky, sage burning on the ground, all around. A large shadow from above crosses over them.

"Don't be afraid. It's your turn now." Her father speaks, still turned away from her. The shadow above grows, larger, darker. She hears an ominous sound. "Watch and learn," her father says as his moonstone emits a beam into the sky. Bobbie's father turns to face her and whispers, "They're coming." He smiles wide—too wide—as the corners of his mouth stretch unnaturally to his ears and his chestnut eyes turn black and large. With the rattle of a snakes tail, chills run down Bobbie's spine.

Bobbie screams herself awake and jumps out of bed, thunking into the door jamb of her room, before running for the shelter of her mother. Behind her, the clock on the nightstand flashes 3:00 A.M.

MOMMA

It's been weeks since Crank destroyed her ant farm, but Bobbie still feels the emptiness in her stomach that something is missing. Her mind keeps going back to the water's edge, when in that horrible moment, she tried to find the structure that quickly sank to the bottom. But the lake was too murky and she was busy trying to scoop out whichever ants floated to the top of the water to help save them from drowning.

She did the best she could that day, until the farmer and his dog came upon her to find her sobbing, cast sopping wet, frantically trying to splash the ants out onto dry land. He coaxed her to come out of the water and took her and her bike back to her mother. Her only solace was she knew the remaining ants could float to the top of the water in little air bubbles and link onto each other by connecting their legs, forming a sort of raft, which could easily float to the shore, as they worked together to save themselves. The alternative was too much to bear.

Now, she lies on the soft ground on top of the hill by her house under an old cottonwood tree, arranging rocks into a makeshift solar system to keep her mind off her intrusive thoughts. She places the stones, perfectly, by size. She's memorized the order of Mercury, Venus, Earth, Mars, Jupiter, Saturn, Uranus, Neptune, and Pluto. She has chosen the best stones, with the best striations and colors to mimic the planets she studies in her picture books. She has them all assembled into a perfect pattern.

A few drifts of cottonwood have landed on her planets, like tiny fluffy visitors not unlike miniature dandelions. She blows them away. Then, a few more arrive. She looks up to see cottonwood confetti, blown from a nearby tree, drifting in the air like springtime snow.

A few yards away, Norma removes their clothes from the line to avoid the nuisance of having to shake the fluff off the freshly dried garments. She waves to her daughter and Bobbie waves back. Norma swats the flurries away from her face, and coughs as she pats her skirt pocket, looking for her inhaler.

Bobbie continues playing by tracing an infinity sign in

the dirt with her finger. She pretends it's an orbit for a make believe, additional planet, one that's made of moonstone and glows brightly in the night sky. One that finds its place situated fourth in line in Orion's Belt. She traces the path, over and over with her finger, and notices a few ants have gathered within the lines, then a few more, and a few more, following Bobbie's orbit exactly.

At this point, cottonwood fairies fall all around, distracting her. She pulls a few tufts out of her hair, and blows the rest away with little puffs and giggles, as some dare to drift back for more. She looks again to her mother. She is horrified to see Norma, collapsed on the ground, her clothes basket spilled nearby. Bobbie runs down the hill to her mother and kneels by her side. Norma wheezes, her throat tightly constricted from a reaction to the cottonwood.

"Where is your inhaler, Momma?" Bobbie pats her mom's skirt pockets. Nothing. She runs into the kitchen and pulls open cabinet drawers. Nothing. She runs to her mother's bedroom and searches the old end table, only to find the drawer is void of anything but a box of tissues and an old bible.

Bobbie screams in frustration as she picks up the handset on the telephone, and dials 9-1-1.

“Please, someone help me! My Momma can’t breathe! Twenty-one-twelve Huckleberry Lane. Hurry!” She leaves the handset hanging by its curly cord and runs back to her mother. Norma’s lips are blue. “Momma, breathe! No! Mommy, please, breathe.” Bobbie drapes herself over Norma and sobs.

Sirens wail in the distance.

THE FUNERAL

A *boom* echoes, sending shivers through the few mourners who have gathered around Norma's freshly dug grave. The sky looms over them, heavy, dark and rumbling—a thief of joy, not allowing one speck of goodness to filter through. Bobbie stands motionless, a chill up her spine with each click, click, click of Norma's casket being lowered into the ground. Surrounding her are her teacher Mrs. Johnson, Farmer McElroy, Clarence his dog, the elder and Noah. They are the only people in Bobbie's life she really cares about. The only ones brave enough to stand in a continual rain, creating a protective barrier around a little girl who has lost everything.

Bobbie is numb, having no more sobs to swallow as she has used them all up. She attempts to take a step forward, toward the grave, but leans frozen—her foot stuck to the earth, like in her nightmares. Noah takes her by the hand and gently guides her forward, until, together, their toes near the edge of the rectangular hole dug into the earth. Side by side the two friends stand as one. Noah drops a little woven heart into the grave and steps back, hanging his head, so utterly sad for his best friend. A red-shouldered hawk flies out from one tree to another.

Bobbie stands at the edge of the grave, holding the hawk quill given to her by the elder, looking small and delicate, oblivious to the conversation behind her.

"Poor child. She's an orphan now," the teacher whispers to the farmer, who nods his head. Clarence lies down, sad-eyed, resting his snout on his paws. Animals always know.

The elder speaks. "She is not an orphan, she is Caddo. The Nation will raise her."

Bobbie drops the hawk quill into the hole. The feather gently floats down and as it rests on the casket, thunder *booms*, unleashing a torrent of rain. It's only natural that heaven should cry on such a horribly, terrible, awful day.

CADDO NATION

Magic fire, blown by a Shaman, sends glowing embers floating through the air. They gently rain down all around Bobbie as she sits, stoic, on the ground, in the center of a Caddo Nation mourning ritual.

Seven solemn weeks have passed since the death of Norma—since the Nation adopted Bobbie as one of their own. "With time and patience, we will help relieve you of your grief, Little Moonstone," the elder—now her Elder— had told her when she first came to live with the Nation. "We will teach you how to walk through life along with the spirit of your mother and father, In'a and A'a. To show you they are always with you, forever in your heart and mind. You can summon them any time as they are never truly gone. Now, you must work to heal your heart wound and grow strong, as you are protected by the great Caddi Ayo, and destined for greater things."

Natives dance as earthy and intimate drumbeats resonate all around Bobbie. She sits in the center of a healing circle where five large stones surround her like a protective barrier;

each stone is carved with a different symbol. The Elder stands close by as the Shaman's voice rises, chanting an unfamiliar song. Somehow, Bobbie understands as she watches the Caddo translate the story, mesmerized by their movements, all accentuated by the hiss of the shakers in their hands, made from rattlesnake tails. Their chests bear designs, painted in blue, with five graduating lines, stacked to form perfect triangles, celebrating the scar beneath Bobbie's collarbone, in their own special and deliberate way.

Bobbie wipes tears from her eyes as the drums soften to a quiet cadence. The Elder approaches—in her hands, burning sage and a wand made of hawk feathers. She prays over Bobbie.

"In'a is with you, Little Moonstone. Her blood runs through you. Her spirit is a part of you now, a part of all of us. She exists in the trees, the mountains, and the great water. Mother Earth sleeps with her memory." The Elder wafts the smoke toward Bobbie with the wand of feathers. " Listen to the wind, Little Moonstone. Hear In'a—her stories of wisdom. From the moment Mother Sun awakens until Father Moon illuminates the darkness, In'a is with you. Even as she journeys on to the next world, she shares her spirit with all living things, as all living things are one."

The Elder then points to the stones.

"These, are the life blood of this world." She describes the carved symbols in a way Bobbie can understand.

The first stone is etched with a diamond shape. "Yakánu. Generous plants. Sacred beings, provide us with nourishment and medicine. Selflessly giving."

The second is etched with a circle. "Nitch'i. Air, invisible, powerful, shared by all living things, both on Earth and also within the great waters."

The third stone is etched with three wavy lines. "Kuukuh. The great water itself, ebbs and flows in rhythm, to connect all things, to quench and cleanse our bodies and our spirits."

The fourth stone is etched with a square. "Hunä:na. Mother Earth. The keeper of all spirits, the source of all that is, and all that ever will be. Our provider of the very gifts of life, water, air.

The fifth stone is etched with five graduating lines. "Taysha…Taysha, means friend. You, Little Moonstone, this is you. You are a friend to all. You possess the power of another world, beyond the stars, and the worlds beyond that. You, possess the knowledge of the great Star People, as you carry the mark."

Bobbie touches her scar as the Elder continues. "You are the chosen one. You must endure your suffering, for your suffering informs you. For it is you who will become a great healer, you who will protect this earth and its people."

Bobbie doesn't understand everything the Elder is saying, but she is grateful for her, for having an adopted family, for not feeling like an orphan, even though she is one.

The drums rise, distracting her from her lonely thoughts, the Elder steps aside and the Shaman reappears in front of Bobbie. One thing Bobbie knows for sure, her life will never be the same, ever again. The Shaman nears the child, holding his palms in front of her in a giving motion. Once again he blows, and fire magically erupts—the light is blinding.

2025

A soft *pop* accompanies the flash of a camera, and a professional photographer directs her subject. “Let’s get one more, Dr. Broadbent, your eyes were closed.”

“Sorry.” Dr. Bobbie Ann Broadbent, smiles, holding a black velvet box, containing the medal she’s received for winning the Nobel Prize in Physiology.

“That’s a lovely ring.” The photographer compliments the moonstone ring on Bobbie’s finger, sitting perfectly sized, her elegant hands no longer that of a precocious child. One more *pop* and the session is done. “There we go. Thank you so much, and congratulations once again.”

“Thank you,” says Bobbie, as she steps down from the platform, making way for the next recipient.

Refined and lovely in a simple black, long-sleeved gown, she exudes style but feels like comfort. Her fiery curls are loosely braided to one side, the thick plait pinned with a crystal brooch—her only adornment. Her elegance is lost on her, as she feels uncomfortable having to have arranged herself for the formal setting. She'd much rather be at work in one of her labs.

She descends the grand staircase leading back into the lavish Nobel reception set in Stockholm City Hall, pausing only for a moment to watch the crowd from above as it hums with the usual murmur of multiple people rapt in polite conversation as they amble about the room. It's not unlike observing a bustling colony of ants, and this thought brings a smile to Bobbie's face as she unwinds the tension in her body she didn't know she was holding.

Bobbie finds her place at the end of one of the long, communal tables, set for her and other prize recipients, and positions her box next to a place card displaying her name burnished in gold. She takes her seat, adjusting herself the way one does at an event where they know no one. The chair next to her is empty. She reaches over to read the name on the place card belonging to it, and smiles, knowingly. She sets the card back to its rightful place, above a gold rimmed china setting. A server fills the empty cut crystal flute at her place setting with champagne, as well as that of the woman seated across from her, who nods at her with a smile, as the table is too deep to start any meaningful conversation.

"Dr. Bobbie Ann Broadbent?" A voice asks, from behind.

Bobbie stands and turns to greet the military man and shakes his outstretched hand. "Yes."

"Congratulations on your most stupendous award."

"Thank you. Congratulations to you too, Lieutenant."

They stare at each other for a long moment, then hug tightly.

"Bobbie, it's so good to see you."

"You too, Noah."

"Come here often?"

They both laugh like they were kids again, playing on the banks of Caddo Lake. They take their seats at the table and smile at each other, each auditing the other's face, trying to recognize the child absorbed within the adult. Noah's freckles, although lighter with age, are a dead giveaway. The pattern of the Big Dipper is still splattered on his cheek. His eyes, still the kindest she ever did see. Noah leans in and bumps her shoulder with his, just two old pals playing the grownup game.

A server breaks the intimate moment, setting an artistically arranged plate of food in front of Bobbie.

"I hate these things," Bobbie, says.

"Architectural appetizers?"

Bobbie chuckles. "Unnecessary ceremonies…all this pomp after circumstance."

They both scan the grandiose affair. Ostentatious arrangements of exotic florals release an array of lilting scents. Table upon table of expensive place settings clink with the dinner service, presented by a tuxedoed staff. Champagne flows and caviar is abundant. The honorable guests are fellow scientists, chemists, authors, philanthropists, physicists, and medical doctors. All take turns genuflecting to the King and Queen of Norway.

"I hear you," Noah says, leaning into his plate. "But it's not every day one wins a Nobel Prize." He grimaces at piled cubes of fish. "However, it's a far cry from Texas barbecue."

"I'll say." Bobbie selects a piece of fish with golden chopsticks.

"Have you been back? To Uncertain?" Noah asks.

"Not really." Bobbie smells the fish and places it back on her plate, opting for a cubed beet instead.

"Yeah, it seemed that when your mom passed, you up and disappeared. My only friend, gone in a flash." Noah smiles, melancholy, and Bobbie can feel the ache in her heart.

"I'm sorry." Bobbie searches Noah's eyes, trying to detect any hint of trauma. Wondering if when she left, he became the brunt of Crank and Harley's jokes. She doubted it, as Noah was always confident in himself. "I still own the house, though."

Noah nods. Surveying his place setting, trying to decipher which utensil to use first. "And your dad? Did he ever turn up?"

"No, neither dead nor alive. Biggest mystery in

Uncertain."

"Hmmm…" They pause for a minute, feeling sorry for the childhood they lost, not growing up together. Noah breaks the ice. "Look at us! Old friends, seated next to each other once again. Just like in Uncertain Elementary…and out of all the people here…it's serendipitous!"

Bobbie rolls her eyes. "The world isn't magic, Noah." Noah stares at her, with deep sincerity. It makes Bobbie uncomfortable—her own pessimism, but she stands her ground. "It's just a seating chart, nothing more."

"Hmmm...we'll see about that." Noah skewers a fish cube with his fork. "I'll tell you this much, I'm not letting you disappear again."

"Cheers to that!" Bobbie says, raising her glass a little too excitedly, catching the attention of the woman seated across the table from her.

"Did you say something, dear?"

"No, no, sorry." Bobbie looks at Noah and they giggle

like kids, once again.

THE DROWNING

CAMP DAVID, CATOCTIN MOUNTAIN PARK, MARYLAND

A woman screams at the edge of a pool, not knowing how to swim, she watches helplessly as a child's motionless body lies at the bottom of the deep end. Two Secret Service officers run out of nowhere. Officer Smith jumps into the pool, diving deep to pull the boy up out of the water, while Officer Morris speaks into his sleeve.

"Send the ambulance around, *stat*!" He turns to the nanny who is sobbing and shaking. "What happened?"

"We were inside, playing hide and seek," the nanny begins. In the background, Smith lays the boy on the ground to begin CPR. "I lost track of him. Searched inside for a while."

"How long?" Morris writes into a small black book.

"About fifteen minutes. Maybe twenty? Until I noticed the sliding door was open. Oh, God!" The woman loses it, falling to her knees, burying her face in her hands. Morris turns to see two paramedics enter with a stretcher and approach Smith and the boy. As they do, Smith recoils, stumbling back away from the boy, a startled look on his face.

"What happened?" Morris hollers to Smith, noticing his partner's distress. Smith appears to be in shock. Suddenly, the boy sits up, dazed, and the nanny runs to his side. Morris approaches Smith, snapping his fingers in front of his partner's frozen face. "Smith! What happened? Did you perform CPR?"

"Uh…I…I didn't need to."

"What do you mean you didn't need to?"

Paramedic One examines the boy's hands, and his severely shriveled finger tips. "Looks like he's been under for quite a while."

Smith, just shakes his head. "I don't understand."

Paramedic Two holds a stethoscope to the boy's back. "Vitals are fine. Lungs sound clear. Let's take him in for observation."

The paramedics wheel the boy off, and the nanny follows

behind.

“What’s gotten into you, man?’ Morris asks Smith.

Smith, a whiter shade of pale, looks as if he’s seen a ghost.

POH

Bobbie's scientific work is projected behind her onto a big LED screen as she sits on stage in a blue velvet chair, being interviewed by a moderator.

"—and so, from our studies of cyanobacteria and oxygenation, combined with that of adrenergic receptors, we're able to develop POH, pre-oxygenating hormone."

"Remarkable!" The moderator turns her attention to the audience. "Are there any questions?"

Noah sits among a sea of fellow journalists, equally in awe of Bobbie's work. Several raise their hands, and the moderator motions for one to stand.

"Uhm, yes, Dr. Broadbent, can you explain, one more time, in layman's terms—for us 'normies', how your pre-oxygenating hormone works?"

"Sure. It's actually very simple when you break it down." Bobbie rises to make her point, adjusting the vest of her smart plaid suit. She clicks a small remote, which changes the images behind her. "Cyanobacteria happen to be the oldest known fossils on earth. Three point five billion years old, to be exact. These bacteria are the ones responsible for the Earth's atmosphere being oxygenated—because it wasn't always. This happened during the Archean and Proterozoic eras, mind you. That's way before 'normies' walked the earth.

The audience laughs at her air quotes.

"So, in studying them and pulling from them and applying what we know of the human body, we've created a vaccine that, when injected into humans, can release a type of adrenaline that immediately allows the human body to be able to produce its own oxygen—all without having to utilize lung function."

The audience murmurs. A woman with a pencil skewered into her topknot calls from the crowd, "Don't you think it's dangerous to be injecting humans with this type of thing?"

"Not any more dangerous than the typical vaccine. Chicken pox. Polio. Diphtheria. Have you had those?"

The woman nods.

"Now, just think of what POH can do for those suffering with, say, asthma." Bobbie pauses. She'll never outgrow the trauma she suffered watching her mother die of an asthma attack. Her life's work has been dedicated to this, so no child, nor adult, will ever have to suffer that fate again. "Picture this. A child or adult is overcome with a severe asthma attack. Their breath becomes scarce. It's shorter, constricted, they start to feel a heaviness in their chest. The heaviness becomes pain as they cough and wheeze. Adrenaline sets in. What do they normally do in this instance? Reach for an inhaler to relax the muscles of the lungs, right? What if they can't find their inhaler? Or they forgot to bring it to school or work? What happens then? They panic, constricting their muscles even more. Making it even harder for them to breathe. They're suffocating. It's terrifying."

Bobbie scans the crowd, "Statistically speaking, one twelfth of you, right here in this audience, suffer with asthma." People in the audience nod.

"Now imagine knowing a person suffers from asthma and

is given the vaccine at a young age…or any age, for that matter. Now when their breathing becomes strained and their chest tightens, their adrenaline intuitively kicks in. When this happens, POH is activated, and their body automatically sends oxygen to their cells, into their blood stream. And this is all done outside of the lungs, so they don't need to inflate at all."

The crowd murmurs.

"Once the body's receptors normalize, muscles relax, the lungs relax, and the attack is over. No inhalers needed."

A man calls out, "Where can we sign up?"

Bobbie smiles. "Typical development time takes four to ten years. We are now in our tenth and last. We're at the end of phase three of a very specialized testing. We should be ready to roll in just a few weeks."

A bell sounds, cueing the moderator to end the session. "Well, that's all the time we have, folks. If anyone has further questions, you can inquire at the press table, out in the hall. Thanks again, Dr. Broadbent, for your amazing contributions, and congratulations again, on your well deserved award."

The audience stands, offering a resounding applause that vibrates through Bobbie's core. Her smile hides the sadness gripped tight to her heart.

THE PLANE

Bobbie contemplates the rain droplets drumming against the window of the airplane. She studies the abstract shapes made as one droplet drips into another, and another, joining together as one impulsive form. There is no thought, just union, an unexpected family.

The plane has been grounded for quite a while, and all she wants to do is get home. She checks her watch again, wondering when they will be free to leave. The only thing she hates more than flying in a thunderstorm, is being stuck in a plane on the tarmac during a thunderstorm.

As she adjusts the air regulator above her head, constricting its intrusive stream, the captain finally garbles a message over the intercom.

"Ladies and gentlemen, this is your captain again. We've just been cleared for takeoff and should be above the storm in no time. So, sit back, relax, and enjoy your flight to Dallas."

A flight attendant leans in smelling like patchouli and cedar. "Can I get you anything Dr. Broadbent?" The striations in his eyes remind Bobbie of the planet Mercury

“No, thanks, I’m fine.” Bobbie pulls a blanket up to her chin and closes her eyes. She dreams of Norma.

NIGHTMARES

A child again, Bobbie is surrounded by a foggy mist, as she stands on tippy-toes in her bedroom, drawing ants on the walls with a blue crayon. A crash from the other room startles her and she drops the waxy stick, running out into the hallway where the fog is even more dense, making it hard for her to see. She hears her mother gasp and wheeze from the other room.

"I'm coming Momma," she says, trying to part the thick, cloudy air with her arms.

Her feet slosh through a sticky liquid, making it hard for her to advance. As she tries to lift her legs, strings of goop pull her soles to the floor, slowing her down. She is desperate to reach her mother. The harder she tries, the more stuck she feels. She follows the dreadful wheezing sounds into the kitchen, where Norma lies on the floor, fighting for her breath like a fish out of water.

Bobby lumbers through the liquid over to the kitchen cabinets, swatting the fog out of the way so she can see. She frantically opens drawers looking for Norma's inhaler, but the drawers are filled with blue crayons—drawers and doors are filled to the gills. With each one she opens, more crayons tumble upon her. Norma gasps behind her.

"I can't find it!" Bobbie wails, fighting her way through the sludge to get to her mother. "Momma!" She falls to her knees and clutches Norma, whose lips are blue. "Mommy, breathe! Momma! Nooo, Mommm! Somebody help me!" she screams.

Bobbie awakens to the flight attendant, hand on Bobbie's shoulder. The attendant leans in close and smiles a bit too wide, mouth stretching horrifically from ear to ear, and with the rattle of a snake's tail, the attendant's eyes turn large and black.

Bobbie jolts awake from her nightmare, the flight attendant's hand on her shoulder. "I didn't mean to startle you Dr. Broadbent. We've landed."

BETRAYAL

PLANET HESPERUS — OUTER SPACE

A galactic storm brews in outer space, fed by the power of a violent solar wind. The sky churns, angry with the ire of some unforeseen god. Below, the beginnings of an impressive space city stands silent, construction halted by the threatening tempest. An ominous derecho broods overhead, harboring strobes of lightning. Every flash within the giant cloud reveals a glimpse of its belly, full with liquid, impatiently waiting to drench the world below.

Astronauts Bing and Sheffield race on a buggy across a rocky terrain, avoiding the geysers that belch all around them, unearthing unknown substances from their cratered openings. The astronauts swerve to avoid being destroyed by the violent eruptions in order to carry on with their mission.

Their destination is a miles-wide lake, spanning the length of the horizon and framed by naked mountains void of any living thing. The only movement: the mechanics of heavy, futuristic equipment as it pumps a thick, blue substance into the vast reservoir.

The astronauts hurriedly exit the rover, grabbing their gear, each taking their post in a different position.

“Let’s get this in the can, before the storm ruins our samples.” Bing instructs Sheffield, through their communications caps.

“Copy that.” Sheffield takes a knee at the edge of the lake and scoops the sticky goop into glass vials, sealing them, and placing the vials into secure slots in a metal container.

Bing, a few yards away, adjusts a pulley attached to a tall metal structure, trying to outpace the cloud looming over him. As it moves in, he can feel the weight of the pregnant mass. He knows it’s only a matter of time before she opens up to soak the terrain below. Bing quickly adjusts the line, fighting to keep his footing against the wind, careful to maneuver the equipment above, careful to do his job the way he’s been trained.

The derecho bursts with an echoing *boom*, startling Bing.

He looks up as clear, gelatinous drops fall from the atmosphere.

"Shit." He wipes his face shield, repeatedly, with one hand, smearing the substance across his visor, trying to see through the jelly, careful to not let go of the pulley in his other hand.

Lightning strikes.

"Jesus!" Bing jumps, fumbling an attempt to secure the line as it slips through his slick gloves. The sheer mass of the equipment on the other end is too much, too heavy, and it crashes into itself. Bing doesn't see the damage it's caused above.

Meanwhile, Sheffield rushes to the rover and places the vials containing the fluid samples into a lockbox, holding his body at an angle to gain leverage against the raging winds. He secures the box and radios Command. "Sheffield to Base Station. Samples are secured. Returning to Civitas I."

Sheffield pushes through the gale, trudging through the storm as if in slow motion, knowing they need to finish their tasks quickly, as he and Bing are in danger. Lightning *explodes*, hitting the equipment near Bing, causing a huge piece of metal to come free from its previously damaged post.

"Shit! Bing!" Sheffield yells as he hears the groan of metal, and watches the large beam swing down and into his unknowing compatriot.

He moves to Bing as fast as he can, wiping slime from his visor as drops fall from the sky. He turns Bing over.

"Fuck."

Bing is unconscious, and the polycarbonate of his face shield has a gaping hole in it. In seconds he will be dead, as the vacuum of space will draw all of the oxygen out of his lungs. Sheffield drags Bing toward the rover, trying to keep his grip as he slips through the slick terrain. Once at the rover, Sheffield hoists his friend up, pushing him to maneuver his body onto the seat.

"Let me go," Bing mumbles.

"Wha…?" Sheffield stumbles back away from Bing. He can't believe his ears, nor his eyes. Not only is his friend not dead, he…breathes? Time stands still as Sheffield's brain catches up to his eyes, making sense of the situation..

“It's okay.” Bing reassures Sheffield, who stands, stunned, as Bing removes his damaged helmet in space, letting it fall to the ground. Sheffield is frozen in confusion. Bing approaches him and places his hands on Sheffield's shoulders—as if to reassure him. He looks deep into Sheffield's dilated eyes and says, “I'm sorry, buddy.” Bing quickly pops the vacuum seals on Sheffield's helmet.

“What are you doing?” Sheffield screams, fighting Bing off, trying to hold on to his own helmet. Trying to hold on to his life.

The men struggle in the storm. Bing yanks Sheffield's helmet off and Sheffield falls to his knees, his mouth wide open, as all the oxygen is sucked out of his lungs. His eyes, even wider, bulge in terror as his eyeballs redden from the blood vessels erupting beneath—a bloody show of fireworks burst within white. He is dead within fifteen seconds.

Bing places Sheffield's helmet over his own head and locks it in. He then attaches his old, broken helmet to Sheffield's suit. He hoists Sheffield's body into the rover, battens the equipment, and activates communications. "Bing to Base Station, there's been an accident. Over."

He drives off toward base.

DALLAS

Bobbie drops her suitcases on the floor in the foyer of her condominium, happy to be back to her familiar surroundings. She'll tend to the unpacking later. Right now, she needs to decompress. She kicks off her shoes and slides her feet into a pair of fuzzy slippers waiting by the door.

"Ahhh," she sighs, closing her eyes to the comforts of home. It's good to be back. To Bobbie, travel is exhausting. Plus, it's not easy being an empath, taking on the energy of everyone and everything.

She reaches into one of her totes and carefully pulls out a plastic container, small and rectangular in size—shaped much like an eight-track tape from the eighties. As she carries it through her condo, soft lighting automatically illuminates, glowing just enough to be welcoming, guiding her through her space, revealing the open floor plan.

Her place, a page ripped out of some futuristic Architectural Digest, is decidedly sparse and designed in monochromatic shades of warm grays and soft tans, reminding her of the color of the velvet that adorns the antlers of a noble buck.

In the kitchen, Bobbie opens a cabinet door—sleek and clean-lined, echoing the style of her living space. Behind the door, a small built-in refrigerator. One not meant for food, but meant to house vessels, much like the one she carries. She sets her container into the refrigerator and closes the door.

"Nimbus, set a timer for three minutes."

"Three minutes. Starting now," a soothing robotic voice coos.

Bobbie opens another cabinet, exposing a stocked wine refrigerator and pulls a red from one of the shelves.

"Nimbus, enable view," she instructs, once again.

"View enabled," her invisible butler announces, and automatic shades power up, exposing a floor to ceiling eagle's view of the neon Dallas skyline.

She uncorks the bottle of wine, pours herself a glass, and takes a sip, staring out the picture windows into the dusk that unfolds before her. In the window, she catches a glimpse of her own reflection and smooths her well-traveled hair.

She takes another sip of wine and examines the contents of her actual refrigerator, bare of any fresh essentials to cook herself a decent meal, and grabs an olive from a container to pop into her mouth.

"Three minutes complete."

"Thank you, Nimbus."

Bobbie takes one more sip of wine and places her glass on the onyx countertop, removing the container she popped into the refrigerator three minutes ago. She carries it into her living room, where she stands in front of a large glass wall. Like the windows to the outside world, this wall is also floor to ceiling and spans the width of her apartment. But unlike the windows, it doesn't look out onto the city. Its purpose is for something completely different.

She peels a piece of adhesive plastic from one end of her container and inserts the newly open end into a slot in the wall.

Slowly, ants begin to crawl out of the container and into the environment behind the glass. She places her full palm onto the glass, and the wall softly illuminates, revealing a colossal ant farm, built into the space, bustling with tens of thousands of ants. Those nearest her palm appear drawn to her and travel toward her as if to say, "Welcome home".

"I've missed you," she says, retrieving her glass of wine and raising it to her friends.

NEWS

Bobbie clicks away on her laptop, tucked comfortably into her bed, unable to sleep from her travels abroad. For her, the jet lag is always the worst part. It's hard enough for her to sleep with frequent, recurring nightmares, never mind the changes in time from country to country disrupting her whole schedule. She plays a soothing game of solitaire as her television silently broadcasts the local news in the background.

She called the lab on the way back from the airport, telling them she'd be working from home for the next two weeks. She asked that no one call her, and no one should be expecting her. She'd call them. She figured she'd be able to catch up on her work, and her sleep, by then. She is truly exhausted, both physically and mentally.

It's been nonstop brain power, developing POH over all these years. With many trials and failures behind her, and then finally, a lucky break. But the real work is yet to begin. She knows once the vaccine is approved for public consumption, the press will be calling and the nonstop junkets will start. She'll have to attend press conferences and doctor conferences and governmental agency briefings. Two weeks of catch-up is suddenly seeming like not enough time.

Out of the corner of her eye on the television, she sees a national correspondent interrupting with *breaking news*.

"Nimbus, turn up the volume."

"—yes, Ed," the anchor is heard mid-sentence, "we're told the president's youngest grandson is stable now. He was heroically saved from drowning while vacationing at Camp David. It seems, he slipped away from his nanny during a game of hide and seek and fell into the pool without her knowing. Luckily, the secret service was on the scene and jumped into action just in time to revive the boy. We're still gathering information, but for now, everything seems to be OK. We'll have more for you after the break. Back to you, Ed."

SITUATION ROOM

SKY RANCH — SEDONA, ARIZONA

General Leonard Saltzman, a hulk of a man, resembles a human bulldog as he looms at the head of a large conference table wearing a tired-of-the-bullshit expression. Around the table, highly decorated military officers silently fill the seats along with Secret Service Agents Smith and Morris. No one dares speak in the Situation Room, as there is a…situation.

Multiple flat-panel screens simultaneously display various news broadcasts from all over the world, announcing the same breaking news about the near-drowning of the president's grandson.

"Goddammit!" Saltzman slams his hands on the table, electrifying the somber mood. "Can we keep anything from leaking to the goddamn press?"

"Sorry, General," Smith apologizes.

"I don't need apologies, Smith, I need goddamn loyalty."

"Yes, sir."

"What is this? The eighth grade? Bunch of gossipy little girls, trying to be popular?" The two female officers in the room exchange glances. "Feeding information to these piranhas?"

No-one says a word, afraid of the *Saltzman stare*. Morris finally mans up.

"We believe it was the nanny, sir."

"I don't give a shit if it was the goddamn Queen of Sheba. I don't want anyone talking to anyone."

"Yes, Sir."

"If the president has a goddamn ingrown hair on his balls, it doesn't get out. Do you hear me?"

"Yes, sir," the group mumbles.

That's not enough for Saltzman, who cocks his head and raises a hand to his ear. "I said. Do. You. Hear. Me?"

"Yes, Sir!"

Saltzman shuffles through the classified papers in front of him and sets his gaze at the lone doctor at the opposite end of the table. The doctor squirms in his seat like an apprehensive child in the Principal's office.

"This is who we need to call?" Saltzman asks, never averting his steely gaze.

"Y-yes," the doctor's voice cracks, "yes, General." His eyes nervously dart at the others seated around the table, as everyone else's are upon him.

"It's not normal to bring a civilian into this environment, Doctor. And highly risky."

"I understand." The doctor tugs at his collar to free his Adam's apple. "But we need her, to help with the narrative."

Saltzman huffs and reluctantly presses a button on the intercom in front of him. "Retrieve Doctor…" —the General refers to his notes— "…Bobbie Ann Broadbent."

"Yes, sir," a voice replies, reverberating around the room, humid with emotion. "When would you like her here?"

"Goddamn yesterday!" Saltzman barks.

Another officer enters the room, and rushes over to the general with a file in his hands. As Saltzman opens the file, stamped red with the words Top Secret, the officer bends down and whispers into the general's ear. The others in the room exchange glances.

"When?" Saltzman asks.

"A few weeks ago, sir."

"And I am, just now, being informed of this? Who's running that shit show up there?"

"Sorry, sir?"

Saltzman shoots a *stare* at the officer, who quickly stands at attention. The general pages through the report outlining an accident in space, mumbling to himself. "Astro-brats…lack of oxygen killing their goddamned brain cells." He rubs his forehead, then grabs a pen and scribbles something onto the file handing it back to the officer, who hurries out of the room.

Saltzman looks out at all eyes, transfixed upon him. "Gentlemen, I hope you brought your goddamn toothbrushes and teddy bears, it's going to be a long night."

DEBRIEF

BASE STATION — CIVITAS I — PLANET HESPERUS

Bing peers through a large plate glass window at Sheffield's bloated and lifeless body, splayed out on a medical examination table, while doctors in white hazmat suits buzz around thc dcad astronaut.

"Bing! Are you with us?" A stern voice, snaps him out of the scene.

Bing turns his attention back to the two senior officers sitting in front of him. They are perched behind an elevated bench, not unlike that of a judge's roost in a courtroom. They stare at the astronaut, who sits in a chair, facing them, in the small sterile room.

"Sir," Bing states with the cold metal heart of an android.

Senior Officer One clicks a remote, and the view of Sheffield through the window disappears behind frosted glass. A large monitor off to the side hisses with a snowy picture. He turns that off as well. “Let’s get through this debrief. It seems the storms have impaired our visual comms, and we don’t have eyes on what happened. Just to clarify, Commander, Sheffield was at his post, adjusting the equipment, when the sky-beam dislodged, damaging his extravehicular visor?”

“Yes, sir. His visor was damaged, and he suffocated before I could reach him.”

Senior Officer Two types notes into a futuristic pad, as Senior Officer One continues. “What was your position at the time of the accident?”

“Approximately five yards east, sir. I was securing the aquatic samples.”

“Hmm. We’ll take your word for it, as we have no visuals to corroborate. Is there anything else you’d like to add that we haven’t covered?”

“No, sir.”

“Very well. The storms are only getting stronger. Got about thirty days until they pass. Civilian missions are halted until further notice."

Bing nods.

"Let's get you back to The Ranch for a decompress. That'll give you time to organize the colonizers and get them up here. By then we'll be ready for you."

Bing nods.

NIGHTMARES

"Bobbie Ann..."

Young Bobbie pushes her way through wheat, following the haunting call of her mother.

"Bobbie Ann..."

"Mommy? Where are you?"

The reeds multiply around the child as a muffled drum beats its rhythm in the distance. The stalks grow taller as they fatten up, pushing in on her small body.

"They're here, Bobbie Ann..."

"Momma, who's here?" she calls, struggling to part the thick vegetation with her arms. "Momma?"

"I'm over here. Don't be afraid."

The drumbeats grow louder.

"Over where?" she calls, swiveling her head, looking for the mother she misses so much. Tears blur her vision as she desperately swims through stalks.

"Momma? Are you still here?"

The crops surrounding Bobbie morph into smooth,

glowing reeds. Fiberoptic strands, radiate blue and sparkle like micro-crushed diamonds.

"Momma? Momma, don't leave!" Bobbie panics, her feet heavy as she trudges through the sticky substance.

The stalks begin to sway, pushing her along with them. They shush and whoosh, back and forth, like sea anemone underwater, parting just enough to give the child room.

"It's okay, child, take my hand." An outstretched arm pushes its way through the anemone. "Don't be afraid."

Bobbie takes her mother's hand and Norma's face appears through the brush. The drumbeats stop. Something is off. Something is missing. Her mother's once-sparkling eyes are no more. Her irises are black, as if her pupils have consumed them. With the rattle of a snake's tail, her mother's mouth stretches, hideously, ear to ear. Bobbie screams and lets go, stumbling backward, disappearing into her surroundings.

Bobbie jolts awake from her dream, finding herself on her living room floor, hair sweaty and matted to her head, just like when she was a child. She looks around her dark apartment, gathering her bearings, hugging her arms around herself for security. They feel wet. Her palms, they are glistening and dewey. She runs her hand across the back of her forearm and rolls the silicone-like liquid between her fingertips. She touches her fingertip to her tongue; it has no taste.

"Nimbus, what time is it?"

"It's three A.M. Would you like me to play some meditation music?

"No."

WAKE UP

Meditation music softly resonates throughout the bedroom as Bobbie sleeps, head under her pillow—a downy attempt at blocking further intrusions into her REM cycle. Her open laptop sits on the bed, still blazing with yesterday's research.

Exhausted from her nightmare, she fell into bed feeling as if she'd traveled into another dimension as if she'd actually been a lonely, frightened child once again. She'd awakened, confused, covered in sweat and dewy from the anxiety brought about by the stress of being a lost child, still longing for her mother, still searching for a message that never quite gets delivered, not to mention the recurring image of the face she sees much too often. It's not human, with its unnatural Cheshire grin, painfully stretching its skin from ear to ear, if there were any ears to be had. And the eyes, large, oddly shaped, consumed by onyx—pitch black and unsettling. Intensely terrifying.

Lying peacefully now, she can be nothing but grateful it was only a dream. Now would be the time to catch up on some much-needed sleep, if it weren't for her phone rudely ringing on her bedside table.

With a groan, she instructs her assistant, "Mrmph, mrmph, mrmph…" Nimbus doesn't recognize her voice, muffled under the pillow, and she tosses it aside. "Nimbus, answer the phone," she mumbles, eyes still closed.

The music is replaced by the caller's voice. "Hello? Bobbie?"

"Mm-hm. Who's this?"

"It's Noah."

Bobbie opens her eyes and smiles at the ceiling. "Mr. Serendipity."

"Are you a believer yet?"

She sits up and pushes her matted hair away from her face. "I'm a scientist, so…"

"Right," Noah interjects, "then let's plan something tangible. I'm headed to the Beanery. Meet me there? My treat."

"Now?" Bobbie hops out of bed to check herself in the

mirror. Her hair resembles a bird's nest someone's lit on fire.

"Unless you have other plans."

She frowns at her reflection. "Ugh, give me thirty."

COFFEE

Butterflies lilt among the flowers of the well-cared-for vegetation planted around the back patio of the Beanery, a quaint coffee shop nestled in a quiet, artsy, part of town. Bobbie and Noah sit at a small table under tendrils of sweet blooming wisteria, its aged stalks so strongly wrapped around a wooden trellis they've twisted the support beams driven deep into the earth. A few other patrons amble about, minding their own business, cradling their locally thrown clay mugs of steamy slow-drip coffee, adrift in their own daydreams. Among the other tables, a couple is rapt in quiet conversation, and a woman in headphones types chapters on her laptop, unaware of the green matcha froth lining her top lip. Everyone is in their own, self-important universe.

Bobbie pushes her sunglasses up into her messy bun and stifles a yawn.

"Rough night?" Noah asks.

A server sets an artisanal coffee and muffin in front of Bobbie. "I didn't sleep very well." The server nods at Bobbie with a smile and leaves. Bobbie lifts the mug, comfortably warm in her hands, and inhales the calming scent of vanilla and sweet cream. She takes a sip and closes her eyes.

"It's the little things, huh?" Noah asks as he tosses a tiny piece of muffin to a bird, perkily hopping under a nearby table, in hunt of some abandoned crumbly morsels. "I can't believe it's been thirty years."

"I know. I'm so sorry I haven't reached out. I've just been..."

"You've just been saving the world," he replies, proudly. "I've been following. It's been fascinating."

Bobbie blushes, embarrassed by the compliment. "Thanks." She fiddles with the paper around her muffin. "I've been a terrible friend, Noah."

"No, you haven't. I have a phone too."

She smiles, grateful he wasn't going to make her feel any worse than she already did. Noah had always been in her corner, protecting her, ever since they were kids.

"So, you're a journalist." She smiles. "I thought, maybe, you'd be off on a boat somewhere."

"I was. Navy had me afloat for three years. Then, three years shore duty. Then USC for journalism."

"Good for you. Married?"

"Never. I haven't stayed in one place long enough." A familiar glint of mischief in Noah's eyes—the shape they make, the quick flinch of his lower lid—brings Bobbie right back to their childhood. "You?" he asks.

"No," she chuckles, "I haven't been out of the lab long enough."

The friends sit silent, comfortable, as familiar as an old married couple, and as if no time at all has passed between them.

"Have you seen the news about POTUS's grandson?" Noah asks.

"I have."

"I was privy to a phone interview with the nanny, early this morning. She was pretty shaken up. Horrified she let the kid out of her sight. Swore she double checked the doors were locked."

"I can't imagine," Bobbie says. "How awful. The secret service saved him, right?"

"Yes. Nanny didn't know how to swim, so the agent pulled him out of the water."

"How long was he under?"

"They believe at least fifteen minutes. At least that's what they've calculated from any security footage."

"And he survived? Does he have brain damage?"

"He has nothing. Kid's fine."

"How is that even possible?"

"The agent pulled him out of the water, and within seconds, the kid sat up. Scared the shit out of the guy." Noah reaches into the inside pocket of his jacket, "Didn't even perform CPR." He pulls out folded papers and hands the report to Bobbie.

"What am I looking at?" she asks

"Information. From the kid's medical records. Scan through his list of vaccinations."

From a file labeled Patient X, Bobbie runs down the complete list of vaccinations from past to most recent. The most recent one…three letters, POH.

"What?" She can feel her cheeks flush pink, knows her neck is too.

"It appears little Danny…the asthmatic…was vaccinated with POH."

"These trials…names are coded…no one knows the identities of who gets the vaccine and who gets the placebo. Where did you get this?"

"I have my intel. Helps being a military man…and also charming." Noah raises his eyebrow.

Noah's lowbrow attempt at humor is lost on Bobbie. "Dammit, this isn't good."

"I think of it as an asset." Wink, wink. He stays in character, but she's having none of it. Noah lowers his head in defeat, amateur comedy career over before it even began. "Bobbie, don't worry. This is me you're talking to." He flicks off an ant that has crawled onto his forearm. Bobbie's eyes follow the insect to the ground as Noah continues, "Do you think he survived because of your vaccine?"

"That's not how it works," Bobbie says, eyes still on the ant, where a few more have ambled to join around a used coffee stirrer, abandoned in a small puddle of spilled cream. "Can't be. Absolutely not." One ant trudges through the liquid on the ground. "I don't know. Maybe?" Bobbie's eyes search Noah's. "POH…that's not the intent…"

"Ho-ly shit," he says, sitting upright.

"Who knows of this?" she asks, concerned, holding up the paperwork.

"I'm guessing only higher-ups, those with clearance."

"This can't get out, Noah. Not now. There are already people out there protesting other vaccines. We're almost at the finish line. Any of these…rumors, will only scare people, set us back to square one. I can't have that happen. This is my life's work we're talking about."

"I understand, completely."

"Shit." Bobbie glances back at the ants on the ground. The little bird has hopped over to peck at them, and she shoos the bird away.

"You, okay?"

"Do you have time to come with me? I want to show you something."

"Absolutely."

Bobbie signals to the server. "Check, please."

FORMICIDAE

Noah can't believe his eyes. His jaw unhinged as he stands, dwarfed, in front of Bobbie's wall of ants, dumbfounded by the sheer size of it all. He scans the ten-by-twelve glass structure, mesmerized by the activity bustling inside.

"Ho-ly shit."

"Maricopa Harvesters," Bobby proudly announces, as if she'd birthed them herself. "Busy little Formicidae. I love watching them work, digging their highways, harvesting their seeds. They even bury their dead. They're a productive little community."

Noah nods as he watches them work, his eyes not knowing where to land as he searches for the tasks Bobbie's listed. Bobbie gently runs a finger along the glass, and Noah is dumbfounded. Are his eyes playing tricks, or are they actually following her? He shakes it off.

"And unlike the benign sugar ant you flicked off your arm at coffee this morning, these ants can kill you."

"What?" Noah unconsciously takes a half step back.

"It would take a hundred stings or more, but it is possible."

"That's not something I'm willing to find out."

"Did you also know, ants can survive underwater for quite a long time? Some, as long as fourteen days?"

"I did not."

"It's true. Ants, like many insects, breathe through specialized openings in their abdomens. An ant can close these spiracles during submergence in water, and also lower necessary bodily functions, entering a torpor-like state."

"Human words, please."

"Sorry. A lethargy. Basically, everything shuts down."

"I'm trying to wrap my head around this."

"POH creates a similar reflex in humans. During an asthma attack, with its particular adrenaline markers, while the body is busy oxygenating the bloodstream, other functions slow, including heart rate and lung expansion. Actually, the lungs don't expand at all, but the paralysis last only a few seconds." Bobbie chews on her bottom lip. "Did the boy have any water in his lungs?"

"I don't think so. None to speak of."

"Hmmm. If the lungs don't expand, there's no vacuum to take in any liquids."

Noah begins to realize his friend's vaccine is even more special than initially believed to be. "Bobbie, this is amazing."

Bobbie turns to face Noah, searches his eyes for the promise she is about to make him agree to. "Please, Noah. Don't break this story. Don't tell anyone about it. Not yet. Do what you can to keep it under wraps, and I'll make it worth your while."

"Don't worry about me," he reassures her. "But let's hope you get your approval before someone else makes the connection."

SURPRISE

On a stool at her kitchen counter, Bobbie's reads in the dark, her face aglow, huddled over her laptop as she scrolls down the page. On the display, an in-depth, scientific study about the survival of ants underwater. It's one of the studies she used when first formulating POH.

She sits up straight and stretches, arching the stiff from her back, bending her fingers backward on each hand before returning them to the keyboard where she clicks a different tab, revealing an empty search bar. She types: *recurring nightmares*

"Fear and anxiety," she whispers to herself.

She types again: *3:00 A.M. symbolism and significance.*

The results touch upon *ghosts and spirits…working hours of the gods…transitions between life and death.* Goosebumps speckle her forearms. She brushes them off and scrolls for more. *In Pythagorean numerology, three is the perfect number. It represents communication. Messages from beyond.* Another chill.

Bobbie clicks back to the original tab, with the study. She raises a clear glass vial from the counter and holds it up to a light. In it—ants, trapped underwater. She can hear Noah's voice as if he were standing next to her, "—security footage shows at least fifteen minutes."

"Could it be?" she whispers. She uses a small strainer to fish the ants out of the water, and gently taps them into a new, dry container, replacing the lid. "Sorry, guys. I won't put you through that again." She watches, making sure the creatures are okay. "Nimbus, dial Noah."

"Dialing Noah."

Noah's phone rings. His groggy voice answers. "Hello."

"Hey," she says, "sorry for calling so late. Meet me at my place tomorrow morning. Maybe we can work on this together. Make a plan to get ahead of the story, talk to people about POH…on my own terms."

"I'll be there."

"Great, sweet dreams." Bobbie slaps her laptop closed. Her phone rings. "Nimbus, answer the phone." A kinetic static fills the room. "Hello?" She calls. "Hello?" There is nothing.

She doesn't see the gloved hand reach from behind. She only smells the overwhelming chemical-doused rag before her world goes black.

SKY RANCH

SKY RANCH — SEDONA, ARIZONA

Heat rises from the pavement under the brutal Arizona sun. Gaseous, transparent waves emanate from the ground, obscuring the scene behind them like a wet windshield in a downpour. It's nature's way of painting an abstract interpretation of reality.

Agents Smith and Morris flank General Saltzman as he waits on the sidelines of the secret runway. The one that delivers only those with the highest clearance, those who have sworn themselves to silence, and those who deny Sky Ranch even exists. The top secret government aerospace facility, nestled between the majestic orange mountain ranges of Sedona, Arizona, hosts only those most trusted in the highest military and government organizations. That is, until today.

An SUV emerges through the vapor, revealing itself in all three dimensions. The vehicle—windows black as night—stops in front of the men and the back door swings open. An agent dressed in black, from sunglasses to shoes, emerges from the back seat. He has a gentle grip on his passenger's upper arm as he escorts her out of the vehicle.

Bobbie yanks her arm away from the man and shields her eyes from the bright sunshine, trying to focus on this unfamiliar scene, still groggy from her chloroform cocktail. The general nods, and the agent is back in the vehicle as it drives away, into obscurity, leaving Bobbie standing there.

"Welcome to Sky Ranch, Dr. Broadbent."

"Some welcome," she complains, more aggravated than afraid. The ground rumbles, and a plane takes off in the background, sending dust and wind their way.

"I trust you've had a good trip?" Saltzman yells over the roar of the engine.

"Only if you consider being kidnapped good," Bobbie yells back, holding her hair to prevent it from whipping her face.

"You've been briefed?"

"Yes, but I'm still confused as to why I'm here."

The general gestures to the SUVs behind him. “Let’s get back to the compound. We can talk there.”

Bobbie scans the Situation Room, with its multiple futuristic monitors attached to steely-gray walls. It's a large, impressive space, with a huge oval table fit for military from around the world. The *tick tick tick* of the general's vintage watch sounds abnormally loud, adding to her splitting headache, making it hard for her to focus on Saltzman as he begins his explanation.

"My apologies for the way we've brought you here, Doctor," he says. "But we couldn't take any chances by giving you advanced notice or location."

Bobbie nods, trying to look like she's got it all together, but her disheveled hair betrays her.

"I hope you know, you can leave at any time, and will not be detained against your will." The general presses a button on the intercom. "Send Dr. Broadbent's belongings to her room." He releases the button and continues, "However, we would like you to stay for a bit."

"And why would I want to stay anywhere I had to be

shanghaied to get to."

"Because we know how much your vaccine means to you."

Bobbie is taken aback at the mention of her vaccine. "What does my vaccine have to do with any of this?"

"Just give us a few days, and you'll understand. We want to work with you, not against you."

Bobbie rests her forehead in her hands and rubs her aching brow. She feels sick to her stomach.

"For now, let's see you to your room. Get some rest. We'll send in some food and water, and something for your headache."

Bobbie stares at her suitcases propped on the floor in the middle of the room provided to her. “Pfff…” she hisses, sarcastically thanking her kidnappers in her mind as she ogles the bags, still packed from Sweden. They took those right along with her. At least she’ll have a change of clothes for the morning, however unbefitting the wardrobe may be.

Still woozy from the chemicals in her body, she sits on the small bed—mattress firm and militarily made, with its sheets and blanket tucked tightly into hospital corners. Her surroundings resemble what she would imagine to be a dormitory on a spaceship. It’s extremely clean and sleek and white, but not too stark, for the soffits in the ceiling emit a soft glow. Her aching, tender head buzzes along with the neon in the silence.

She lies back on the bed, trying to ease her pain, but that proves to be a mistake. The room spins as if she’d come home drunk from a wild night out with friends. Something she never did, because her head was always in a book, or her computer, or in a lab doing the research for POH.

Unable to control the spins, her nausea bubbles up from inside, and she barely makes it to the bathroom before throwing up in the toilet—releasing both bile and nerves. She lowers herself to the ground and rests her forehead on the cool tile floor.

I just need a minute.

THE VACCINE

Bobbie rummages through her suitcase, looking for something to suit the Sedona weather. She is wrapped in a towel, fresh out of a much-needed shower. What kind of kidnappers have the mind to take the victim's luggage right along with her? She'd slept in the clothes she'd arrived in, the night before, too hungover from being drugged to even attempt pulling her clothes over her head. She didn't remember leaving the bathroom and falling onto the bed, but seems to have made it through the night without any nightmares. And for that, she was grateful. She pulls out a pair of linen slacks and a coordinating top and slides them on. Hand in her suitcase, she pushes the box aside—the one containing her Nobel Medal, and fishes deeper into the jumbled clothes until she finds it. Her father's moonstone. She winds her fingers around the smooth orb, which is cool to the touch.

She lifts the stone from the bag and holds it in her hands, rubbing its smooth surface to calm herself. It's been her security blanket and talisman of sorts ever since Norma's death. She contemplates the sphere for a minute, becoming lost in its iridescent layers, which morph and change as she turns it in her hand, pulling her deeper into its center, calming her.

The *buzzing* of her phone startles her, snapping her out of her meditation. She sets the stone on the nightstand next to a half-drunk glass of water and two empty packets of ibuprofen.

"Hello?"

"I'm at your place. Where are you?" Noah stands outside of Bobbie's apartment with his phone pinched in the crook of his neck and a coffee from The Beanery in each hand.

"Ugh, Noah. Something came up. I'm not there."

"Obviously." He takes a sip from the little hole in the top of one of the coffees. "Did you hear?"

"Hear what?"

"Are you near a television?"

Bobbie scans the futuristic room. A flat screen is mounted above a floating console. "Yes?"

"Turn on the national news."

Bobbie approaches the buttonless monitor, feeling around

the sides and behind it for a way to turn it on. She finds nothing. A singular drawer floats on the wall beneath the monitor, but it has no pull, and she can't pry it open. She pushes on the front of the drawer, and it slowly pops open, revealing a remote control. She grabs the remote and presses the big red button. *Some things never change.* The television clicks on, and she scrolls to a major news channel. On the screen, a serious brunette in a cobalt blazer stands outside of a building that looks all too familiar—it's Bobbie's apartment. The anchor continues her report from the street. "…POH, developed by Nobel Prize laureate Dr. Bobbie Ann Broadbent, has finally passed its ten-year trial. This is great news for asthma sufferers. Additionally, success of the vaccine is projected to alleviate a majority of the eighty-two billion dollars a year spent treating the disease. We are told, POH will soon be available through doctors' offices and pharmacies across the United States. Stay tuned for more details. Back to you, Ed."

"Congratulations Doctor Broadbent!" Noah beams. "The timing couldn't be more perfect. Wouldn't you say?"

"This is great news." However great the news, she finds it hard to celebrate in her current situation. "I…I really can't believe it."

"Incredible news. We need to celebrate." He pauses. "Where are you, anyway?"

"I'm actually—" *Click.* The phone goes dead. "Hello? Noah?"

She hears a knock at the door, and the general peeks his head in. "You ready for a field trip?"

Bobbie nods without saying a word; she'll call Noah later. She slides her phone into her pants pocket, her feet into her loafers, and follows the general out. As she leaves the room, she doesn't see the news ticker crawling across the bottom of the television screen. *SOURCES: PRESIDENT'S GRANDSON APPARENTLY VACCINATED WITH POH. MORE AT 11:00.*

Bobbie double checks her seatbelt as she's jostled in the back seat of the convertible jeep bounding over rugged terrain, on what appears to be a dirt road leading directly into the side of a mountain. General Saltzman, a mound of a man, takes up the front passenger seat, as Morris drives, silently, sitting erect, both large hands on the wheel positioned at ten and two, in full control of the situation. Bobbie can feel his gaze on her from the rearview mirror even though she can't see his eyes behind his dark aviators.

She pulls the neckline of her shirt up and over her mouth and nose to prevent the Sedona dust from entering her lungs and turns her head to the side to protect her eyes. In the distance, she sees something that makes her heart jump. An abandoned Indian reservation sits tucked in a gulley between two rusty mountains. In the camp, an old fire pit, dug into the ground, sits abandoned and brittle, its flames extinguished a long time ago. But in her imagination, an explosion of glowing embers swirls around her like confetti in the air, transporting her back to her youth, back to the memory, where the flames burned much higher than her small body.

Adult Bobbie watches herself as a young girl on her adoptive reservation. Her freckled, tawny skin and explosion of curly red hair, stands out among the Caddo's rich, warm skin and jet-black hair. They surround her, welcoming her, healing the pain after the death of her mother. Encircled around the fire, they dance and sing the songs of their people, energetic flames reflected in their eyes. In unison, they raise their arms to the night sky.

Young Bobbie turns to her adult self. "They're here," she whispers. Bobbie feels a chill run up her spine, and just like that, her memory is extinguished, along with the flames of long ago.

"Congratulations surely are in order, Doctor!" Saltzman yells over the wind. "Heard about your vaccine's approval. What a goddamn glorious achievement!"

"Thank you!" she yells back, shifting her eyes to the rearview mirror, where Morris's sunglasses have not moved.

"Almost there, sir," Morris exclaims as he maneuvers the jeep up the side of an orange mountain and toward an entrance that has magically revealed itself.

OPERATIONS & TESTING

The jeep pulls through a hole in the mountain and into a massive space, resembling that of an airplane hangar that's been plucked from the future and tucked inside the mountain. It's vast and appears empty, save for a few armed guards who have taken their position at the entrance, which has, once again, disappeared behind rock. Morris opens the door of the jeep for the general, and Saltzman steps out to open the door for Bobbie.

"Follow me." He shows the hint of a smile—however it is a grumpy bulldog smile—in anticipation of giving a tour.

Bobbie follows the general while Morris stays behind. Their footsteps echo as they approach two armed guards dressed in fatigues, stationed in front of an entrance into who knows where. The guards move aside, allowing Bobbie and the general passage through two massive doors. The doors slide open and they step through, into darkness. The doors close behind them, and Bobbie can't see a thing until a series of lights click on in succession, illuminating the passageway before them.

"Just a few more steps," Saltzman says as he leads

Bobbie to yet another set of doors—these, unattended.

The doors open, and a rush of cold air hits Bobbie in the face, almost taking her breath away. She wasn't ready for the change in atmosphere—a one-hundred-and-eighty-degree pivot from the blazing temperature outside. Sure, Arizona was dry heat, but it still felt like sticking one's face into a preheated oven. Now, it was like they were being chilled in a meat refrigerator.

Before Bobbie, an arched silver hallway spans far and wide as sheets of pristine metal are formed into a polished dome enclave, beckoning her and the general in. She wonders how on earth such a thing was constructed, because she can't identify one seam or rivet in the smooth walls. In all her years she had never encountered such a space.

"Welcome to Sky Ranch O&T, Doctor."

"O&T?"

"Operations and Testing. You are in one of the most, if not *the* most, highly classified locations in the world."

On either side of the hallway, large plate glass windows

curve up the walls, in the same sweeping way as the metal sheets, giving Bobbie a firsthand view into bustling labs, and testing facilities. Through one window, scientists peer into microscopes while others type into futuristic tablets as unidentifiable machines spin and whir. Through another, a doctor in a white jumpsuit injects something from a syringe into a man's arm, also dressed in white, while others stand in line, awaiting their turn. The general knocks on the window, raises his closed fist, and the glass turns opaque, obscuring the scene.

"Privacy glass," he says, proudly. "Bulletproof and soundproof."

It's at this point Bobbie notices the silence. Not once did she hear anything from behind the glass. She only thought she did. For the echo of their footsteps fills the hall as they continue to walk past the windows to unknown worlds, where more and more scenes unfold before her like a muted play.

"The most innovative and confidential testing is done here," Saltzman continues.

"Quite futuristic," Bobbie exclaims, not knowing where to look next as they traverse through a honeycomb of hallways—each passageway leading to yet another scientific spectacle.

At what seems to be the end, Bobbie finds herself face-to-face with a gargantuan sentry. He stands stoic near a large glass door. The guard salutes the general and steps aside, revealing a panel with a small round hole. The general approaches the panel, leans forward, and places his right eye in the center of the circular cutout in the wall, where a laser quickly scans his eyeball. The doors slide open, revealing a smaller, all-glass room, and the general steps inside.

"Come on in," he says, "No time to waste."

Bobbie steps inside, and the doors close. The general taps his right temple. "Glass eye," he says. Pointing to the shiny unmoving prosthetic in his head, something Bobbie hadn't noticed before. "One quick scan, and it's my all-access pass to anywhere in this place." The room begins to move, and Bobbie realizes it's an elevator, as red sandstone whizzes by while they descend within the mountain."There are five levels from here on down, and we have access to all of them," the general explains. "We're in the center of the goddamned earth." The elevator slows, stops, and then begins to travel laterally. Bobbie braces herself, holding an arm out against the wall, surprised at the sideways movement. "Bet you didn't expect that to happen," Saltzman states sheepishly. " Sorry, forgot to tell you that part. I'm used to it by now. We not only move north to south, but we can also move east to west."

Bobbie notices the general never pressed a button to request a specific floor, as this glass elevator has no panel. There are also no floor numbers illuminated overhead. Instead, symbols flash, appearing on the glass, with each level they pass. If she didn't know any better, she would think they were the same symbols carved on the rocks on the Caddo reservation. She has no time to dwell as there is too much information to take in.

The elevator slows to a stop with an extended *whoosh*, and rock gives way to a three-hundred-and-sixty-degree view, as the glass box deposits the two like the tube in a bank's drive-through window. They are smack dab in the center of a sleek and massive lab buzzing with activity. Bobbie turns in the vessel like a lizard looking out from a terrarium, observing its surroundings beyond the glass. Indistinguishable technicians, covered in white from head to toe, buzz about, overseeing sleek, titanium equipment. The elevator doors open and Bobbie and the general step into the space. He motions for her to follow him past giant machinery that expels a futuristic assembly line, bottling a blue liquid into small, clear vials. At the next station, a whirring machine spins the bottles, tagging them with labels. *What's this?* On the labels are three large yellow letters, P-O-H, and a plus sign.

"What's going on here?" Bobbie exclaims, "Is this… POH?"

As if on cue, the technicians simultaneously stop what they are doing to look at Bobbie, but only for a split second.

"No," says the general. He points her toward a technician,

who drips the liquid from one of the bottles onto a glass slide, examining it under a microscope, and computing their findings. “Go take a look.”

Bobbie approaches the tech. “May I?”

They step aside and Bobbie peers into the microscope.

“Hmm. I see it’s compositionally different. But the markers are there.”

“Let me show you.” Saltzman replies, “Come. Walk with me.”

Bobbie nods at the technician, who continues their work at their post. She follows the general out of the lab.

“I’m so confused as to what’s going on here.”

“Patience.” The general leads Bobbie to another set of sliding doors. The silver plaque to the side of the door is etched with three wavy lines. *Water.* Again, the general peeps his glass eye into an opening and the doors swiftly slide open. Immediately, Bobbie is met with the smell of a high school gymnasium…rubber and chlorine. The room is dark and feels humid, much warmer than any of the other areas on this high-tech field trip.

In the room stands a life-sized cylindrical glass tank—an aquarium, filled with water, and lit with a singular glowing spotlight. The tank appears to span six feet across in diameter and twelve feet high. A man in a white lab coat stands in front of the tank, typing into a rolling, computerized pedestal. There is something inside the tank, but it is obscured by the glass.

"Come closer," Saltzman instructs Bobbie. As she nears the tank, the contents become clearer. Bobbie gasps. A young man is suspended in the water. He floats upward, his ankles clamped in shackles, the shackles chained to the bottom of the tank, preventing him from floating to the very top, where he could easily escape. His eyes are closed, his face peaceful. *Surely he must be dead.*

As if on cue, the young man's eyes snap open, startling Bobbie. A shot of adrenaline buzzes through her body. "He's just a kid. What is this?"

Saltzman points to a digital clock above the tank, the display counts up: 19:02:03.

"Nineteen minutes and counting," he says, "Goddamn kid is breathing underwater, without assistance." The young man gives Saltzman a thumbs up. Bobbie tries to make sense of what she's seeing, as the general continues. "Not POH. POH Plus."

"What on earth is POH Plus?"

Saltzman turns to the lab coat. "Doctor, can you explain?"

"It's a DNA modifier, using epigenetic changes, created to alter the human respiratory system. With these changes, as you can see, humans are able to breathe within oxygenless environments."

"I am well aware of this type of theory, Doctor, as I invented it. Why are you calling it POH Plus?"

The doctor appears shocked and impressed at this revelation—that the inventor of POH would be standing in his presence. His eyes shift to Saltzman, who nods, giving the doctor permission to divulge the information. "We've merged with POH…if you will. Merged it with a composition of our own. In essence, you haven't created a vaccine, you've created a genetic modifier…and we have as well. Together, they make POH Plus."

"So you've infringed on my intellectual property?" Bobbie could feel the red creeping up her neck, ready to flush her cheeks.

Saltzman steps in. "No, they've created their own. Your vaccine is safe, Doctor. POH Plus is not for public consumption. It's for top secret, military use only. It will never see the light of day."

Bobbie's thoughts flash back to the Beanery. She can hear Noah's voice clear as a bell. *"Also…It appears, little Danny, the asthmatic, was vaccinated with POH."*

"And what about the president's grandson? Underwater for fifteen to twenty minutes, and he didn't drown? He wasn't vaccinated with POH, was he?"

"There was a mix-up." Saltzman states, matter of fact.

"Oh my God. How on earth?"

"Not sure. We're investigating."

"You need to shut this"—Bobbie waves her arm dismissively—"this thing, down."

Saltzman barks an order to the heavens, "Can someone turn on the goddamned lights?"

With that, one by one, rows of overhead spotlights illuminate, from the front of the room to the back, immediately implying the scale of the project. For in those few seconds, the room becomes a warehouse, and that one tank becomes hundreds. All filled with young people, submerged underwater.

"I'd say it's too late, Dr. Broadbent. To shut it down."

The red in Bobbie's cheeks travels down her neck, bursting into hives. "Oh my God. Are you kidding me?" She takes in the scene of young people, floating in water, chained to the bottom, timers counting the minutes above their heads. "Have you lost your mind? Are they prisoners? Why are they chained to the bottom?"

"Let us show you," the lab coat replies.

Bobbie, in shock, is unable to compute what she is witnessing. The general takes her elbow and escorts her to an empty tank. A young woman with long dark hair secured into two braids—who looks to be about eighteen—is dressed in a white wetsuit, the same as the rest of the subjects. She climbs down a ladder, into the tank, and makes her way to the center. "They're volunteers. Military," the general explains over the unfolding scene. "If I threw *you* into this tank and locked you in…" The woman steps into the shackles, and they automatically tighten around her ankles. "…and filled it with water…" Water rushes up, into the tank, through the grates in the floor. The woman blows out a series of quick breaths before the water reaches her face. As the water quickly fills the tank, the woman floats upward. "…*you'd* do everything in your goddamned power to swim out of there…" Bobbie zeroes in on the woman's feet, shackled, floating above the floor of the tank, with no chance to escape. The woman appears calm, determined. "She won't."

Saltzman continues. “She’s been trained for this. Prepared for this to happen. The shackles keep her from floating out of the top of the chamber.” The woman gives a thumbs up, and the timer above the tank illuminates: 00:00:01, and counting.

The doctor rolls his computerized pedestal over to Bobbie. Shows her the woman’s vitals displayed on the screen. “She has no fear, Dr. Broadbent. See? Only adrenaline.”

“And with that rush of adrenaline, the modifier takes over.” Bobbie answers.

“Correct.” The doctor types a few things into his computer, bringing up more information. “Her lungs close off, preventing water from entering.”

“She self-oxygenates,” Bobbie says, knowing that is exactly where her vaccine plays a part.

“Correct,” answers the doctor, happy she understands.

“A state of lethargy. Just like the ants,” Bobbie whispers to herself.

“What’s that?” Saltzman asks.

“Nothing.” Bobbie turns her attention back to the woman in the tank.

She seems to be at peace.

Back in the glass box, Bobbie and Saltzman ascend the center of the mountain, red rock whizzing by.

"Concerning the president's grandson," Saltzman states, "we can't kill the story because the goddamn vultures have already sniffed it out—damned if I know how. And once they have it, they pick it to death until all they're left with is marrowless bones. There are going to be questions about your vaccine, and we'll need you to make a statement."

"Me? And what do you suppose I say?"

"We just want you to confirm the child was vaccinated with POH."

"But he wasn't."

"If you say he was, they'll leave it at that. We don't need them digging any deeper. That never turns out well for anyone. We'd be happy to prepare something for you."

Absolutely not! Bobbie thinks long and hard about what she should do. "No, that won't be necessary, I have someone I can call. Someone within the press."

“The press? That’s not happening.”

“Within the press, but loyal to the military.” Bobbie sizes up the general’s suspicious brow. “Look. You,”—she waves her hand—“or your people created this mess. You didn’t have to drag me into it. But now that you have, I don’t trust you won’t smear my good name, or my vaccine, for that matter. I’ve worked too long and too hard on POH to have it all be for nothing. If you want my help—my statement—I’m asking you to let me do it on my terms.”

Bobbie watches the elevens, chiseled in the brow between the general’s eyes release the slightest bit of tension. “Okay,” he says, “bring them in. But if I sense any goddamn monkey business. You’ll both disappear so fast, your mothers won’t even remember they birthed you.”

Bobbie’s heart sinks a little at the mention of her mother. Her stomach aches with a pain that never goes away. It just hides in the shadows, waiting for moments like this. If it weren’t for her beautiful mother’s battle with asthma, she never would have gone on a quest to find a cure, she never would have invented POH.

LUNCH

The scent of the pines—citrus and vanilla, expelled from the hundred-foot trees, wafts through the air, as squirrels scurry throughout their branches, kicking up the alluring aroma. The bouquet is lost on Bobbie as she sits at a table with Noah on a quaint patio seemingly nestled within the forest. She's deep in thought. Noah watches her push lettuce around her plate.

"Hello? Earth to Bobbie. Where'd you go?"

"Sorry," she says, dropping her fork onto her plate and adjusting herself in her seat. "I was just thinking about my mom."

"Oh." Noah knows it's a tough subject. He remembers her sweet mom and how she doted on Bobbie. How she protected her after her father's disappearance.

"Why couldn't I save her? Why couldn't she just live until I became an adult? Until I invented this vaccine?"

"Uh, you were how old? Ten? When she died? That's a crazy question to ask your inner child. Plus, I don't think you would have ever gone on to invent it, had she not."

"How's that?"

"Post traumatic growth. Instead of spiraling downhill, you came to a new understanding of your world and the people in it. You used your trauma positively. You needed to succeed, to survive. You couldn't save your mom, but you can save everyone else."

"It's not going to bring her back."

"Are you kidding me? She is in every molecule of your vaccine. She will be in every person who receives it. Plus, she's always in here." Noah reaches out to touch above Bobbie's heart, and notices the triangular scar below her clavicle. He quickly changes the subject. "So, why have you brought me here?"

"I need your help," she says, lowering her voice, leaning in. "The president's grandson wasn't vaccinated with POH."

"He wasn't?"

"No," she whispers, "they've created a variant."

"Who?"

She looks around the patio, arm-hair on end. No one

catches her eye, but she's suddenly paranoid she's being listened to. "The military," she whispers, "the government. They've basically stolen my vaccine and altered it. They're calling it POH Plus."

"What a bunch of tube socks. They have no imagination."

"They're using it for some sort of underwater testing. Apparently there was some mix-up, and the boy was injected with the wrong thing."

"A mix-up? You mean to tell me, the US military—"

"Shhh…lower your voice."

Noah whispers, "You know who…just happened to lose a top secret formula and inject it into…of all people…the president's young grandson? No way!"

"I don't know. That's not the point. The press thinks he was vaccinated with POH, and the people that be want me to keep it that way. If I'm out there making a statement about my vaccine, then I am the distraction away from what really happened—what's really happening. But I'm not letting them hand me something to read. I need you to prep me."

"Sure. I'm in. Maybe we can uncover what's really going on here."

Bobbie recognizes the look in Noah's eyes, and she already regrets letting him in on it. "Noah, please. I vouched for you. They already don't want you around, so they'll be on high alert. Promise you'll help me with this one thing, and not nose around."

"You know I'm a journalist, right? Did you summon me here to torture me?"

"Just try to stay out of sight, okay?."

"Okay. I'll behave. Where are we going anyway?"

The *thunk, thunk, thunk,* of the road, pounds out a rhythmic cadence as Bobbie and Noah sit silently in the back of the SUV. Smith drives—rigid—his sunglasses watch Bobbie in the rearview mirror. She stares back, annoyed. *What is with these guys?*

"Sorry, Doctor. I'm going to have to blacken the windows."

"It's fine," she says.

A black divider rises between the front and back seats, and the already tinted windows on the automobile become opaque, blocking the outside world from inside the back seat of the vehicle. Bobbie and Noah exchange glances, not saying a word.

NIGHTMARES

Young Bobbie pushes through the illuminated reeds as the glowing strands sway back and forth, shushing and whooshing peacefully, as if they are submerged underwater. A faint drumbeat in the distance grows louder with each sticky step forward..

Bobbie breaks through an opening and finds herself back on the Caddo reservation. Her father stands off to the side, his back to her, his glowing stone raised high to the heavens. A ring of burning sage encircles his feet.

The Elder appears, backed by rows of ancient Peoples Bobbie doesn't recognize as they stand stoic and silent behind the Elder. The drumbeats continue and the Elder speaks, "You Little Moonstone, are the chosen one." The drumbeats grow louder.

Bobbie's father turns to face her. "You're finally here. It's your turn now."

A pinch below her clavicle prompts Bobbie to look down at her triangular scar. It burns bright red.

"You are the chosen one," says the Elder. "They will help

you."

"Who will help me?" she asks.

"Don't be afraid," her father says as he extends his moonstone out toward her. Bobbie reaches for it, but her arm grows, stretches, as her father is pulled farther and farther away from her. Drumbeats grow even louder, quickening their pace.

"I can't reach it, Papa."

"You must alter his path," he continues. Drumbeats even louder, even quicker.

"Whose path?" she asks, confused.

The drumbeats stop. The ground rumbles under Bobbie as she is yanked backward—forcefully—through the glowing reeds, her breath sucked out of her as she falls from the steepest cliff. She is pulled farther and farther, falling, faster and faster, until she hears her father's desperate whisper, "Alter his path!"

She hits the ground.

HITTING GROUND

An angry rumble beckons Bobbie to open her eyes. She sees nothing but dark, endless sky above her, and feels only dewy earth beneath her. She lies on the ground, outside, in the middle of the night, disoriented, awakened from a dream that felt more real than life itself. If she could see her face, she'd notice the texture of the grass imprinted on her cheeks. She'd know she must have been lying there for quite some time.

She pushes herself up, trying to get her bearings. *Alter his path.* Her father's moonstone is in her hand. Confused, she scans her surroundings not remembering where she is. Then she sees it—the building, the one that houses the dormitories. The window to her room is open. She must have fallen out, must have been sleepwalking again, an annoying habit she can't seem to break. She hears a rustle in the hedge behind her.

"Hello? Is somebody there?"

Something rushes from the bushes, startling Bobbie to her feet. She runs into the building, not daring to look behind.

Back in the dorm, Bobbie double checks the window to make sure it's closed and locked, wondering if there are security cameras and if they captured her sleepwalking. Of course there are. This was going to be embarrassing. What a weird experience, this whole thing.

She reaches into her backpack and pulls out the bottle of sleeping pills she packed for her trip to Sweden, and carries it into the bathroom, oddly grateful her kidnappers took her bags along with her.

She shakes a pill, then two from the bottle to ensure she stays put, then pops them into her mouth, and with a palm of water from the bathroom faucet, washes them down, catching a glimpse of herself in the mirror as she does. She almost doesn't recognize herself. The worry etched into her face is something new. Her eyes, dark and anxious, tell the tale of her sleepless nights. Not to mention, she has bruises on her forearms and on her legs as well. She looks as battered as she feels. The general did say she was free to go at any time. She'd leave after tomorrow's press conference

One more check of the locks, and Bobbie slides between the sheets, resting her head on the cool pillow, staring at the moonstone on the end table next to the bed, wishing this whole thing was just one bad dream.

DISCOVERIES

The sun on Bobbie's skin feels like a gentle hug as she soaks in every ounce of it, welcoming the prickle of warmth over her flesh as she sits on the bottom stair in front of the dormitories. She traces an infinity sign in the red, dusty earth with her finger, just like she did when she was a kid. If only she could hear the squeak of the screen door behind her and her mother's quiet footfall once more. Ants follow the shape she makes in the dirt, round and round, summoned by her command. It's the party trick she's perfected over the years, the one she's never shared with anyone.

"Refill?" Noah calls from behind.

Bobbie quickly pulls her hand from the ground and the ants disband."Yes, thanks." She accepts Noah's offering as he fills her empty coffee mug. "I need it today." She's still groggy from the extra sleeping pill she took.

Noah sits down next to her and leans in, saying quietly, "I'm not sure where we are, but I feel like I'm back in my college dorm. If my dorm was clean, and white, and situated on

Mars." Bobbie chuckles, take a sip of her coffee, as Noah continues, "Here. I wrote something for you to say to the press." He hands her a plain, white envelope.

"Thanks."

"Also, I saw something strange last night."

"You did?" Bobbie feels the heat in her cheeks as she's sure he's going to say he saw her tumble out her window onto the grass.

"A big airship."

"Oh." She's relieved he didn't. "Doesn't sound that strange. We *are* situated on a runway. I've been seeing transport planes ever since I arrived."

"No, this was different from a transport plane—from any other plane. The shape was sleek. I can't even describe it." He thinks a bit. "Like an almond, maybe, fatter on one end with retractable wings. It was unlike anything I've ever seen before. And, it was quiet…really quiet. I couldn't hear any engines. I saw it hover to the end of the runway, retract its wings, and then…disappear. Just. Vaporize."

"Hmmm." Bobbie cradles her mug in both hands, wondering what actually is this place called Sky Ranch?

"I ran outside, but there was nothing—no sound, no smell, no lights in the sky."

"You sure it wasn't a drone?"

"If it was, it was the biggest drone in the history of the world."

Bobbie can't focus, her head too fuzzy to wonder just what it was General Saltzman and his cohorts were up to. Instead, she looks off to the majestic orange mountains, longing for a change of scenery. Maybe a different perspective would help. "You up for a hike?"

"Absolutely."

The hoarse cry of a red-shouldered hawk echoes through the canyons, as it circles in a cobalt sky, weaving its way in the sun, casting its shadow upon the rusty Sedona mountains. Dusty, orange trails are speckled with green vegetation in nature's flawless presentation of complementary colors. A multicolored collared lizard suns itself on the rocks, unbothered by Bobbie and Noah as they hike past. They've made it halfway up the mountain and haven't seen another soul along the way, which, they assume, is to be expected in this hidden place. Bobbie wondered if they'd run into a guard along the way, but so far, no one has crossed their path. And for that, she was grateful. Bobbie steps on a ledge and hoists herself up to the next level. Her linen pants, rolled into Bermuda shorts, expose the purple marks on her legs.

"Where'd you get the bruises?"

"Oh, I'm such a klutz," she says, figuring it's not considered lying if even she didn't know what caused them. "I'm always bumping into things. I don't even notice them anymore."

Okay, that was a lie. She stops to tie her undone shoelace. "I miss this."

"Blisters from inappropriate footwear?" Noah says, pulling off a loafer to shake out a pebble.

"No, exploring with you, knucklehead."

"I do too. It's been way too long." They stand side by side on a cliff, looking out over the vast expanse of brilliant red and orange rock. The setting is gorgeous, pristine, untrampled by the masses. Bobbie is overcome with a strong sense of melancholy. "We never had a chance, did we? To grow up together? Once Mom died, I was sent to live with the Elder. It was either that or be shuffled off into the foster system."

"The right choice was made for you. Look at what you've accomplished. Plus, we're together now, and I'm not going to disappear." Noah turns to face Bobbie. She has disappeared. "But you might."

"Noah, over here!" Bobbie calls, excitedly.

Noah follows her voice around a corner. "Wow!"

Bobbie stands in front of a massive multilevel dwelling, intricately carved into the mountainside. Perfectly incised, open-air apartments are connected to each other by stairs that have been hand chiseled from rock, ascending from one level to another. Bobbie imagines how the now-abandoned structure must have bustled with activity in the past, as her eyes travel from doorway to doorway, leading from neighbor to neighbor.

"Amazing, isn't it?" she says, awestruck. "A whole community must have lived in the side of this mountain, hidden from view." She can't help but think of her beloved ants.

"Incredible. I wonder what tribe built this?"

Bobbie has disappeared again. "In here!" she calls.

Noah follows Bobbie's echo and enters through a craggy opening in the face of the mountain. Inside, undulating stone twists and turns, like the interior of a giant conch shell. The walls are smooth and ethereal; sunbeams pierce their way in, through slits high above, casting dramatic spotlights onto the floor of the cave. Bobbie's illuminated hair appears to be aflame, as she stares at the walls before her.

"Look at these." Etchings are carved into the walls. Bobbie studies the ancient representations of natives, trees and animals—etchings that tell the stories of those who existed before. "I think they're Sinagua."

"What's that?"

"The etchings." Bobbie points to the wall. "Look at the representations of pottery here. They appear to have the markings of the Sinagua, an ancient indigenous people."

"I've never heard of them."

"The Elder used to tell me bedtime stories about the many different Nations scattered throughout the country. She used to tell me we were all connected, in one way or another, even though we lived separate lives. I think my dad used to believe the same: that we are all somehow connected." Bobbie looks around, takes in her surroundings. "The Sinagua must have settled here decades ago and built these dwellings." A knowing smile crosses Bobbie's face. "They remind me of the ant farm I had as a child, these tunnels." For a split second she is lost in thought, but quickly comes back to the subject at hand. "The Sinagua must have lived in these mountains for safety and shelter. I remember them specifically because of the lore."

"What lore?"

"They're said to have suddenly and completely vanished."

"Where did they go?"

"No one knows. One day, the Nation was here, and then suddenly gone. Disappeared. Maybe they assimilated into other tribes." Bobbie runs her hands over the squiggly lines—the sign for water. "Sinagua literally means *without water*." She follows the etchings deeper into the cave, where the stories change from the daily life of figures hunting, growing maize, artisanal pottery, to something else….the planets and stars, the constellations, figures that don't look quite human. "Star People," Bobbie whispers to herself. She hears the voice of the Elder. *"We are a conduit to the Star People, Little Moonstone. Although they inhabit the great sky, and seem many worlds away, we have the ability to communicate with them. You must follow suit."* Bobbie moves her hand over the etching of a large oval form, never really knowing what the Elder meant by being able to communicate with other worlds.

"That's it!" Noah says.

"What?"

"The airship…that shape…that's what I saw last night."

Carved underneath the ship was something familiar: five graduating lines, just like Bobbie's scar. "Noah! Look at this, it's just like my—" She turns. Noah stands eerily still, like he's got the most important thing in the world to say to her. "What's wrong?"

Noah pulls his shirt collar aside. Under his collarbone is the same scar as Bobbie's. It takes a minute for her to compute.

"How?"

"That night. Thirty years ago. The flash in the sky."

Bobbie touches her scar. "What are you talking about?

This is from my accident."

"I saw it, Bobbie. That night. The boom in the sky. The horizon glowed. It was awesome."

Bobbie sees herself, a child again, running through the field, toward the glow. She remembers the pull, how it was magnetic, like she had no control over her own body.

Noah continues his explanation. "After your mom died and you were gone, it happened again. I was out on the water, in my boat—the one my uncle helped me build. The sun had just set, and I knew my mom was going to be mad. She didn't want me out on the water in the dark, so I was hurrying to get back to shore. Suddenly, the sky burst into a million colors. Then, something…something sucked me up into the atmosphere. I felt like I was flying and falling all at the same time. Then, it was all a blur." Bobbie can't believe what she is hearing. It was like Noah was describing her experience. "I have nightmares about it, and I know you do too."

"I…I…" Bobbie is at a loss.

"And what about the ants?"

"The ants? What about them?"

"Have they always followed your direction? Summoned by you? Have they always been able to heal you?"

"How did you—"

"I was there. I followed you, that day you ran out of school. The day Crank and Harley were being assholes. I saw you fall, saw you cut your knee, saw the ants make your wound magically disappear. How was that even possible?"

"I don't know." Bobbie's adrenaline buzzes through her body. This is too much information to process. "You have nightmares too?"

"Yes. I'm floating. They're experimenting on me in some sort of otherworld. Then, I wake up exhausted, like I've run a marathon…moisture on my skin. I remember bits and pieces, then nothing at all."

Flashes of Bobbie's nightmares flicker before her eyes like a haunting film reel…the sticky liquid…the pushing her way through. Her mother's face. Her father's face. The horrifying face. "What are you saying, Noah?"

Noah points to the five graduating lines etched into the cave. "This! This symbol, underneath a spaceship. This is us! This is what happened to us! Abducted. Beamed up like Scotty, then branded like cattle, and sent back down."

Bobbie can't look at him, refuses to concede. "That's ridiculous."

"Really? Us both receiving the Nobel Prize is ridiculous! We're just two kids from East Texas." As the words tumble out of his mouth, Noah wishes he could stuff them back in—take the pin out of the balloon of Bobbie's ego. She has, after all, invented a lifesaving vaccine. "Look. I should just speak for myself. You've always been smart as hell, maybe even smarter when they sent you back. And I don't know why they took us, or what they did to us, but they did something." He grasps her shoulders. "They took us, Bobbie…and I worry, they still do." He looks at the etchings on the wall. "Maybe they took the

Sinagua."

She pulls away from his grasp. "I can't with you right now." She turns her back, not wanting, nor ready to face his exhortation.

He follows her. "Don't you remember when we were kids, the day by the lake, you asked me if I believed in aliens?"

"You didn't answer me."

"Why did you ask?" She doesn't answer. "Why can't you stop being a goddamned scientist for five minutes?"

"Because I didn't remember, okay? I was ten and terrified. I saw my dead father, standing there, suddenly alive, and then I saw…something! I couldn't look away. A siren's song in my head, it's like they were calling me. And it was beautiful. Blue. My eyes burned, they glowed so brightly, then, suddenly, everything turned black. Suddenly, I was back home, walking up my front porch stairs, buzzing like I'd been struck by lightning, not remembering where I'd been. I don't remember them taking me. And, I don't see them in my dreams. I see something terrifying, but I don't believe it's them."

"But, there's evidence, right? Bruising for no reason, nightmares, animals behaving weirdly. And why are we here? Together. In this highly classified place, no one knows exists?"

Bobbie doesn't have a good answer for her childhood friend. "Serendipity?"

Noah's face softens with his warm smile. "They're using us. But, for what? That…is what we need to figure out." He turns to travel back up and out of the cave. Bobbie follows. She doesn't want this knowledge—it's too much responsibility. She has so much on her plate right now.

"I just can't, Noah. I'm busy trying to figure out how to save people here. On earth."

Noah stops. "Right! You're right!" He jogs toward the exit. "I think I know."

Bobbie tries to keep up. "Noah! Wait!" Noah's silhouette is stark at the entrance of the cave, backlit by a blindingly bright light. Bobbie shields her eyes from the glare until it disappears.

She exits the cave. The stars in her eyes make it hard for her vision to adjust. From what she can see, Noah is gone. “Noah? Noah! Where are you?”

Bobbie peers over the edge of the mountain, afraid of what she’ll find. There is nothing. Nothing, but the high-pitched cry of the hawk, gracefully circling above.

LIES

Press representatives from around the globe are gathered in the conference room of the luxury hotel located in downtown Sedona. General Saltzman is off to the side, flanked by Smith and Morris, watching Bobbie as she stands at the podium accepting questions after a speech she just gave on POH. Bobbie is there physically, but her mind is on Noah, wondering where he ran off to.

"Yes, it's true, only a very few people know the identities of our subjects, in these blind trials," she continues. "We also cannot divulge identities, due to strict HIPPA laws. In this case, it was leaked that the president's grandson was, in fact, vaccinated with POH, and I have been given permission by the family to confirm that." Bobbie's stomach aches, just saying the words, but, at this point, she will do anything to protect her lifesaving vaccine. She couldn't bear having one more person suffer the loss of a loved one the way she lost her mother.

"Has he been evaluated?" A reporter asks. "Is he doing okay?"

"I've been told he's been evaluated since his accident and has been doing wonderfully. Also, I'm happy to report, he's not suffered a severe asthma attack since being vaccinated. And we are seeing the same results with a majority of our vaccine recipients."

Another reporter asks pointedly, "Doctor, we've heard rumors—rumblings—if you will. Do you believe the POH in the boy's system helped him survive underwater for all that time?"

A blinding light in the back of the room pulls Bobbie's focus. Noah stands, an apparition of himself, an aura of light around him. *Does anyone else see this?*

"Doctor?"

In a flash, Noah is gone.

"Uh…sorry…lung function slows when the vaccine is activated. But, I also believe our heroic secret service agents sprang into action in a timely manner, and the boy wasn't underwater as long as initially reported. I think we should give a hand to agents Smith and Morris for their valiant efforts." Bobbie presents her hand toward Smith and Morris, and the reporters applaud.

Smith nervously tugs his collar as he is brought back to the scene of the accident and his frightful memory. *Smith lays the boy on the ground and leans in to perform CPR. The boy's eyes shoot open, and he smiles, a bit too wide, as his mouth stretches from ear to ear and his eyes turn black, causing Smith to recoil in horror.* Smith wipes the sweat form his brow and gives a half wave as the reporters applaud.

Bobbie continues. "As far as breathing underwater…well, that sounds like science fiction to me." She feigns a laugh, and the reporters laugh with her. Bobbie shoots a glance at the general, who nods with approval, and taps his watch. "It seems like that's all the time we have. Please direct any other questions to my office. Thank you."

NOAH?

Bobbie bursts into Noah's dorm room—or at least what she thought was his room. She'd not been in it once since he came to Sky Ranch. He had always met her outside.

"Noah, Noah!" she whispers loudly.

She searches the room, identical to her own, observing the pristinely made bed, military style. She searches the bathroom; nothing is out of place, not even the towel, which is folded neatly, with others, and tucked into a cubby in the wall. She places her hand under the faucet of the small sink. It's dry as a bone. It appears as if no one has ever been there.

"Where are you?"

Back in her own room, she quickly changes into more comfortable clothes and grabs her backpack, stuffing in a light jacket, and her father's moonstone. She sees the envelope from Noah and realizes she never even opened it because she forgot to bring it to the presser. She was late getting back to her dorm after her hike with Noah, and now he's nowhere to be found. She tucks the envelope into her bag, and hurriedly walks out the doors and down the stairs. Saltzman is waiting outside.

"Going for another hike?"

"Yes, I'd like to clear my head."

"I just wanted to say, thank you for your speech. It seems to have gone over well."

Bobbie lets out the sigh she didn't realize she'd been holding. "General, I've had a lot of tragedy in my life and have worked to create something that would prevent others from experiencing the same. I don't like lying to the public. But, now that it's done, I'd like to go home, if that's okay with you."

"We'll get you on a flight, first thing in the morning."

"Thank you."

"Enjoy your hike."

Bobbie walks away, thankful to be going home tomorrow. But she has more thing weighing on her mind. She turns to address Saltzman, who is still standing there, watching her leave.

"Oh, General."

"Yes."

"Have you sent Lieutenant Springfield back already?"

"Lieutenant who?"

"Springfield." The General's face is blank. Bobbie presses. "Noah Springfield, my friend from the press. He was here at the dorms, to help me with my speech."

"I'm sorry, Doctor. There hasn't been anyone here but you."

THE CAVE

Bobbie is dwarfed by the abandoned dwelling carved into the side of the mountain. It rises high above her, larger than life. She imagines the Sinagua Indians living there, a bustling community, walking up and down the hand-carved stairs, visiting each other, preparing food for themselves and their neighbors, even tucking their children in on a chilly desert night. She visualizes them, much like she sees her ants in their environment. And she knows that although a differing species, there are many similarities between human communities and those of animals and insects. Bobbie reflects on her immense respect for all living creatures.

It's at this moment she feels sadness the Sinagua are no longer there—their homes abandoned. All that work, for naught. At least they are all gone together. At least they haven't left one woman standing to fend for herself. Bobbie aches with a deep loneliness she hasn't felt since childhood. She misses her mother and father. She misses her ants. She misses Noah.

Noah. Surely the general was mistaken. She saw Noah

with her own eyes, spoke to him, rode with him in the SUV. Smith was there. She couldn't understand, in a place so secretive, why the general wasn't informed of Noah's visit.

She shakes her head, trying to loosen the thoughts crowding her brain, trying to delete them altogether as she enters the cave.

Once again, she studies the etchings on the walls, illuminated by ribbons of sunlight splitting through the rocks above. Running her hand along each carved shape, she follows their progression, pressing the pads of her fingertips in between the grooves, feeling the depth of the carvings and wondering if they've eroded much, over the years. Would they disappear one day too? Just like the Sinagua? She touches each one, like a blind person reading braille, until she gets to the last etching—to the five graduating lines, the perfect triangle, just like her scar. The one Noah confessed he also had. Did she imagine that? And, where did he disappear to? She was going to give him an earful, tomorrow, when she was finally back home.

She notices something she hadn't seen before, probably because she was distracted by Noah's story. Another opening sat just beyond the etchings. She ducks into the entrance, following it deeper into the belly of the mountain, following, until the walls close in, until the ceiling gets lower and lower, making her grow taller and taller, like Alice in Wonderland. She walks the path until there is but little light. She wonders if this is how her ants feel, traveling through their tunnels. Maybe she should turn back —there won't be much more to see without a flashlight.

But a low incandescent glow beckons her in. *Just a few steps farther.* She has one more opening to squeeze through. She gets down on her hands and knees and pops her head through the hole. It's a cavern, with enough space for her to stand, and light enough to see. She pulls off her backpack and pushes it through the small opening, then crawls through to the other side. She rises and brushes the earth from her knees. The room, soft and glowing, feels like a womb protecting its inhabitant. She notes primitive pieces of pottery scattered about, and the walls…they are lovely. Milky. Iridescent. If Bobbie didn't know any better, she'd think them moonstone—exquisitely opalescent. The space calms her. In its center, a body of water reflects colors, much like that of an oil slick in the rain.

Bobbie sits at the edge of the water, cocooned by the cave, and opens her backpack, removing her father's moonstone, comparing it to her surroundings. Legs crisscrossed, she holds the stone in both hands, breathing deeply, eyes closed—meditating—relishing this feeling of serenity, hidden away from everyone and everything, completely taking advantage of the effect this unfamiliar space has on her. And, it's not just her. The stone glows, not exactly like it did when she saw her father hold it up to the heavens, but more gently. Dizzy with the stone's energy, she closes her eyes, and is transported to an *other* place. Somewhere else. No longer swaddled in her surroundings, she stands unprotected in the middle of a universe unfolding around her.

The sky is dark, awash with stars and multiple moons. A

voyeur, she watches another version of herself as a child, standing on the rocky terrain of some new planet, in her shattered glasses and outer-space pajamas, hair billowing in the breeze…slow motion. Something stands next to young Bobbie. Tall. Blue. It lifts an arm to point in a direction, to show the child what it wants her to see.

The child watches a military space rover, built like a dump truck, back up to some sort of conveyor belt, pitched forty-five degrees up into the air. When the truck reaches its mark, the back bed slowly rises upward and its gate swings open. Blue, jelly-like masses, similar to the one standing next to young Bobbie, begin to fall from the truck onto the conveyor. "No," the child says, with tears in her eyes, the scene reflected in her shattered glasses. Deceased alien bodies travel up the conveyor and fall into a large machine. "No!" the child cries out as the machine grinds and whirs, pumping a bluish-green slime, through a spout on the other side. The substance falls into a body of the same, where two astronauts are crouched along the shoreline, scooping it into glass vials.

The child turns to Bobbie, "Make them stop!"

Bobbie opens her mouth to speak to her younger self, but nothing comes out as the ground rumbles under her feet and the rover barrels toward her!

"Stop!" Bobbie yells. Bringing herself out of her vision and back to reality, back into the cave, where the walls are made of moonstone and the ground rumbles under her, for real. If only she knew what was happening five stories below.

THE LEGION

Five Stories Below…

In a cavernous underground facility, a large, transport vehicle filled with passengers rumbles by a legion of armed soldiers standing at the ready.

Bing watches closely as young civilians in white jumpsuits form lines in front of a massive video display screen. They are mesmerized by a promotional commercial touting a new civilization on another planet. On the screen, a woman in sleek, futuristic attire, lauds a brand-new life on Planet Hesperus.

"Welcome to Hesperus," she says, in the overly calm, saccharine voice of an artificially-intelligent infomercial presenter.

The projected movie depicts a pristine, blooming utopia, with pink skies, clear water, and lush vegetation. A hybrid bee-butterfly playfully flits across the screen. The young people, mostly dark haired with golden skin, stand, hypnotized, as the woman continues.

"You have been chosen to be the first colonizers of this

free, new world. A world that offers you a fresh start. Where space is plentiful, disease does not exist, and the global atmosphere is pristine."

The white jumpsuits look at each other and smile, flatly, robotically. Absent are the crinkles in the corners of their eyes.

The presenter continues. "Upon arrival, you will be escorted to your new, comfortable dwellings. Anything you desire will be at your fingertips as you populate this brand-new world."

A scan of the crowd reveals mostly-blank faces, mouths turned upward, eyes void of emotion. Except for one person, whose eyes betray them. Whose irises are dilated, sharp, and darting, revealing a sense of terror. The booster shot they were given hasn't worked completely, their thoughts not controlled one hundred percent. Tiny beads of sweat percolate near their hairline, and as one droplet connects to another, a single bead rolls from above their temple, down their cheek. As they lift their hand to wipe it away, they are quickly met by three soldiers. For any hint of independent, negative emotion, is not allowed. The soldiers quietly drag the frightened recruit away from the crowd —which remains unmoved, unbothered by the sprag of their boots along the floor.

BING

Bobbie picks a pebble from the treads of her shoe. She is back in the situation room with General Saltzman. Still in her tank top and pants from hiking, she came straight away, once she emerged from the cave and saw all of the general's missed calls and messages asking her to meet as soon as possible. He said it was urgent…had something she needed to know. She was hoping it was information on her flight back home tomorrow.

The *tick tick tick* of Saltzman's watch echoes in the quiet space as he looks over the file in front of him, huffing and puffing like a man who is irritated with everyone. Bobbie doesn't know what to do with herself as she runs her tongue along her teeth, still gritty from her dusty hike. Finally, Saltzman speaks.

"It seems they're pausing underwater testing," he says to her, flatly.

"Thank God," she says, relieved by the news. However fascinating, she thought it was an awful idea to begin with.

"God has nothing to do with this," Saltzman says as he presses a button on the intercom, "Send him in." The door opens and Bing enters, carrying a silver briefcase. "Dr. Broadbent, I'd like you to meet Commander James Bing. Bing is one of our brightest and most progressive astronauts. A doctor of planetary science, he commandeers Civitas I, a ship that's part of our newest and most classified space program.

Bobbie stands to shake Bing's hand. Bing simply nods, without eye contact, without saying a word, and sets his briefcase down on the table. She returns to her seat, eyeing the general, who has his gaze set firmly on Bing. Bing pops open his case, revealing a small but complex computer. As he types, video images from space appear on the large glass presentation wall.

Bing begins. "Thirty years ago, we discovered Hesperus, a young planet hidden within our solar system." A planet populates the screen, then zooms out to show its exact location. "You can see it here, within the Orion constellation."

The fourth star! Bobbie feels the hairs on the back of her neck stand up as she remembers lying on the blanket as a child and noticing the extra star in Orion's belt.

Bing continues. "On Hesperus, the soil is dry, but nutrient rich, and we have access to an anaerobic aquatic source. Over the years, we've had a skeleton crew working in conjunction with our base station in space. The highly skilled crew has been able to construct a city, in what we deem the first interplanetary state. It's about the size of Texas. We will populate the city, and more developments will follow, until we eventually colonize the whole planet. "

"How will you do this?" Bobbie asks, not knowing why she is privy to this information.

"The Legion. We've a trained army and thousands of civilians ready for duty. Some boarding transport ships as we speak."

The screen switches to a large, convertible transport vehicle carrying one hundred young people in white jumpsuits. It makes its way up a ramp and into the belly of an enormous space plane, where one hundred seats await, each equipped with a launch entry suit.

"In no time, the Legion will be dressed, and flown from Earth to Hesperus, with me at the helm."

"Where will they be housed?" Bobbie asks.

"On Hesperus, of course."

"How will they survive? All these people?"

"The city is domed, with a manufactured atmosphere." The picture on the screen switches to a cityscape, not unlike that of New York or Chicago, nestled under a giant clear dome. "Unfortunately, the atmosphere is very expensive to maintain," Bing continues. "It's also taxing on the Base Station's solar panels, which, as of now, can't sustain such a large environment. And that threatens the existence of the very thing we are building."

"But they've developed an alternative," Saltzman adds.

"Which is?" Bobbie's stomach feels sour.

"POH Plus,'" says Bing. "It allows us to breathe on Hesperus without the aid of an extravehicular helmet."

Bobbie addresses the general. "The underwater testing?"

Bing answers. "The atmosphere on Hesperus is very much like being underwater. As a matter of fact, underwater testing is more taxing on the body than surviving on Hesperus. Minutes underwater here, equate to years on the planet."

"And you're sending those…kids?"

"The water recruits you saw will be the first earth civilians in space. As we outgrow the city, we'll build more. The planet has plenty of room to expand."

A video of undeveloped terrain unfolds, and Bobbie's heart sinks. She recognizes the landscape from her vision in the cave.

"What about other life forms? If this planet is what you say it is, it must be supporting its own species."

Bing shoots the general a look. "We are still in the discovery phase."

"Meaning, you've discovered life?" Bobbie imagines blue bodies being dumped onto a conveyor and carried to their demise.

"Nothing worth saving," says Bing, callously.

Bobbie's cheeks burn with anxiety. As a Native American, this especially stings. "Commander, are you colonizing a planet that's already inhabited?"

"We've done our testing. Whatever plasmas we've found are vegetative. They have no brains, no nervous system, to speak of."

You're lying. "Certainly all life is valuable." Bobbie looks from Bing to the General, searching for any shred of empathy.

"Yes," Bing replies flatly, "they are useful to us. We've found they are made of a specialized deoxyribonucleic acid. One that contributes as an additive to your vaccine, resulting in POH Plus.."

The goop in the water! "Their DNA? You're using their DNA as an additive?" Bobbie glares at the general, "Did you know this?"

"It's not my job to know how these things work, Doctor. I'm not a goddamned scientist. My job is to protect the program and people of the United States of America."

"By shuttling them off into space? Sending them to replace a civilization that already exists?"

"By doing whatever is necessary!"

"Whatever is necessary? Does that include allowing your '*brightest and most progressive'* doctor of planetary science to commit genocide?" Saltzman stays silent as Bobbie can't stop the words rolling off of her tongue. "Why have you really brought me here, General? Why burden me with this information? I find it hard to believe you would break security protocol, to let a civilian into this god-awful place, just to have me make a statement to the press about my vaccine. What is your real agenda?"

Bing answers for him. "We need you to pull your vaccine."

"What?"

"We need you to pull it from the market."

"Not going to happen."

“We don’t want it out there for other countries to get their hands on it. In no time, Russia or China will discover what we have and try to follow suit.”

“Your theory makes no sense. This shouldn’t be a factor in your race to space. It’s a vaccine. To help save people. Here. On Earth.” She turns to the general. “In the United States of America.”

“You will be saving people,” Bing gaslights. “It’s only a matter of time before Earth, itself, has no atmosphere. This planet is being polluted daily…the oceans, the air, global warming. Do you think it’s going to get any better? This is a chance to create a whole new world. Join us, Doctor. Come to Hesperus and be a part of something bigger and better than yourself.”

“You’re delusional, and I’m not pulling POH.” Bobbie stands to leave—she’s had enough. “I’d like to go home—now.”

“Then we’ll make it fail,” Bing threatens. He types something into his computer, and the scene on the presentation wall changes to a live stream of the president's grandson, playing with his toys while his nanny reads on the sofa near him. "And we'll start with little Danny, here. Let me introduce a real-time presentation of your vaccine. As you can see, the boy is doing just fine. Listed, are his heart rate, blood pressure, blood oxygen level, and so forth. Everything is normal." Bing types again, and the boy begins to cough. He stops playing to hold his chest and a looks to his nanny, who runs to him as he begins to suffer an asthma attack. "Uh-oh. Little Danny's vitals are changing," Bing says, like the serial killer he is.

Bobbie's heart jumps into her throat as she watches the screen, watches the boy's blood oxygen level plummet. "Stop it," she says, watching the nanny search for the boy's inhaler.

"Nanny can't help him because there is no inhaler," Bing lilts as the nanny runs to a phone to make a call while the boy collapses on the floor. "Instead of your vaccine helping him breathe, it will kill him."

"Stop it!" Bobbie protests, knowing it's not her vaccine

in the boy. Adrenaline burns her veins, and an all-too-familiar terror arises.

Saltzman rises from his seat. "Now wait a goddamn minute." This is not something the general knew, or approved of.

"You can't do this!" Bobbie panics, thinking back to her mother, dying in front of her eyes.

"We can, and we will." Bing says, chillingly calm. "You are the only one who can stop this."

Saltzman presses the intercom. "Security!"

"This isn't POH!" Bobbie demands. "This is your mutant formula!"

Smith and Morris enter the room. Bing continues. "Correct. And POH Plus will be in every vaccinated arm in no time. But no one knows that. You've made your statement to the press, confirming the fact the boy was vaccinated with POH. And the boy will die from it." On the screen, the boy gasps, like a fish out of water. "And so will everyone else believed to be vaccinated with POH."

“I’ll pull it! Just stop!” Bobbie screams as she pops up from her chair. The tears on her cheeks make faint tracks as they roll through the residual dust on her face left over from her hike.

Bing adjusts his settings, and the boy regains his bearings —begins to breathe easily again. His nanny scoops him up into her embrace. He seems stunned but okay. Bobbie falls back into her chair, shaking, unable to comprehend the nightmare unfolding before her.

“Are you out of your goddamned mind, Commander?” Saltzman barks.

“On the contrary, General. In my mind, everything is clear as crystal. You see, with POH Plus, we can control every aspect of every organ function in the body, at any time. It creates a much more stable world, this controlled environment. It also creates a much more obedient society.”

BANG BANG

"Smith! Morris! Take Commander Bing into custody," Saltzman orders.

Smith steps forward to apprehend Bing.

"Wait," Bing says, holding up a finger, "let me show you something, Smith." Bing types again, pulling up additional health information on the screen, alongside a photo of Smith. Smith, stunned and confused, realizes it's his own vitals being displayed. He stops and grips his chest as he gasps for air.

"Morris! Apprehend the Commander!" Saltzman orders.

Morris doesn't move as Smith continues to struggle, falling to his knees. Smith's lips turn pale, and, in a split second, they stretch across his face, from ear to ear, displaying a terrifying Cheshire grin, fit for a demon, as his pupils consume his eyeballs, turning them black, right before he collapses to the floor. Bobbie is frozen at the literal sight of the of the nightmarish face that plagues her dreams.

"Morris!" Saltzman barks, propelling himself up from his seat to take care of business, himself.

Morris steps forward and turns toward Saltzman, pulling his pistol from its holster and pointing it at the general. "Sorry, General." Morris pulls the trigger, shooting the general in the forehead.

Bobbie screams, startling Morris who spins around and shoots twice.

The world stops.

In dead silence, Bobbie zeroes in on the barrel of Morris's gun where the bullets leave in slow motion, and head straight for her. Everything is hyper realistic, from the ridges on Morris's knuckles, wrapped around the grip of the gun, to the smooth, shiny tips of the bullets rotating as they hurtle her way. With violence, the sound comes rushing back into the room, loud and clear. Bobbie feels a burning sensation in her chest and shoulder as she is spun around. Her world goes black, and she collapses to the floor.

"You imbecile!" Bing yells at Morris.

"I didn't mean to."

"We needed her!" Bing paces the floor, looks back and forth at both bodies lying in the quickly forming puddles of their own blood. "Argh! Maybe we don't. Get rid of the bodies, quickly, you stupid fuck."

"Yes, Commander."

Bing kicks Smith's body hard, causing the fallen agent to groan. "Get up!"

DUMPSTERS

A lazy sun takes her time setting behind the mountains as she casts her somber glow along the pavement, far behind Sky Ranch. It's funny how nature continues to be beautiful, even during the ugliest of scenarios.

A black SUV quietly rolls in and pulls up to two dumpsters, side by side. In the distance, a forklift empties a third, spilling its paper contents into the belly of a large incinerator.

Morris emerges from the passenger's side of the SUV, and a woozy Smith gets out of the driver's side. Morris opens the back hatch, and the two men struggle to hoist the sizable body of General Saltzman out, up, and into one of the open dumpsters. Both men push his body, rolling it over the metal edge until he falls in with a thunk. Next, they pull Bobbie from the back and throw her on top of the general, along with her backpack. Morris closes the lid.

"They'll be incinerated in no time."

Smith nods and climbs back behind the wheel while Morris slides into the passenger side and slams the door shut.

They drive off into the sunset…a not so happy ending.

Blood drips from a drainage hole in the bottom of the dumpster and onto the pavement, still bathed in the glow of the setting sun. Ants begin to gather around the tiny crimson puddle.

PULLING THE WOOL

THE LEGION

Bing arrives at Legion headquarters in an SUV chauffeured by a Legion soldier. The soldier opens the door for Bing, and he exits the vehicle with a calculated coolness that never breaks. Like nothing ever happened. Like he didn't just aid and abet in the murder of General Leonard Saltzman.

Dressed in his flight suit, Bing hands his helmet to the soldier. "Take this to the ship."

"Yes, sir." The soldier takes the helmet, and scurries off, unaware of the sins of his commanding officer.

In the background, engineers and technicians mind their own business as they man their posts, buzzing with energy in anticipation of the upcoming mission. Bing walks with a hurried determination through the busy professionals, and points to the closest members of his team—which only include two people, as Bing trusts no one.

" At the desk…now," He demands.

Legion flight controllers, Frank Waltz and Anthony Harris quickly follow Bing into the Mission Control Room. They listen intently as Bing rattles off his plan to which no one is allowed to have a contrary opinion. Dwarfed by the giant screens behind him, Bing stands in front of the images of his immediate and future universe. On the screens are independent, live satellite images of Hesperus, Earth, and the inside of Civitas I—the airship he'll be manning.

Mission Control is the place where it all happens—where Waltz and Harris are usually joined by other flight controllers, analysts and engineers to help guide Bing and his ship through space on their journey to Hesperus. But today, Bing has a different plan in mind.

"It will only be the two of you. Can you handle it?"

Waltz and Harris look at each other before hesitantly answering in unison. "Yes, sir."

"Good. Pull up the recruits," he commands.

The men hurry to their assigned seats at the giant desk.

Harris jockeys the video of Civitas I to focus on the center of the ship, where one hundred white jumpsuits sit in their space gear, waiting for their captain to arrive and shuttle them to their new world.

Bing stares at the screen for a long time—long enough for the other men to exchange glances and shrug.

"How do I talk to them?"

"Sir?" Harris asks.

"The recruits, and the crew. How do I deliver a message over the intercom?"

"Just press that button, Commander, and speak into the mic."

Bing presses a button that lets out a high-pitched squeal over all of the speakers at Legion underground. He then delivers a message no one was expecting.

ANTS

Ants congregate away from the puddle of blood coagulating on the pavement, and travel single file, up the wheel and then the corner of the dumpster, making their way into the top of the metal basin.

In the dumpster, Bobbie lies unconscious; a sliver of waning light peeks through the lid and streaks across her face. The ants crawl onto her chest, where two bullet holes—murderous mistakes caused by a panicky trigger finger—reside, side by side, one under her collarbone and the other on the front of her shoulder. The ants march a path in the shape of an infinity sign around the bullet holes, connecting them within the pattern. They intuitively trek, converging together over the two bloodied craters, pierced into Bobbie's tender skin…then apart again. Together, apart, together, apart, a continual pattern until they reveal fresh, pink skin. Until they have healed Bobbie's wounds, her caretakers once again. When their work is done, they follow each other, marching single file, exiting the dumpster like the good soldiers they are, their lifesaving mission accomplished, gone, but never too far.

In the distance, the forklift driver abandons his post and hops off of his equipment, which has run out of gas. It’s too late to fill it now; he’ll be back first thing in the morning.

CIVITAS I

Bing is strapped into his captain's chair on Civitas I, eager to escape before anyone finds out about General Saltzman. By the time anyone has a clue, Smith and Morris will have the mess cleaned up, and neither one will talk because they know with the click of a button, Bing will kill them just the same.

He makes the adjustments on his console, allowing him to be the sole captain of the mission. Civitas I only requires a manned crew of two to make it to Hesperus. And since his copilot Sheffield's sudden—death—Bing has decided to make the journey on his own. He'll leave the recruits behind so as not to tax the ship's life support system, nor deplete the food supply, leaving more for himself as he hijacks the ship to make his departure.

"Legion to Civitas I, how do you read?" Harris's voice is heard over the comms.

"Loud and clear, Legion. Solo controls have been prechecked and Civitas I is good to go."

"Roger that, Commander," Harris replies, with a slight

pause. "Sir, are you sure you want to man the mission alone?"

"Dammit, Legion, that is not a question to be asking now. I'm more than capable of handling this ship."

If Bing had gone through the proper channels, he would not be manning the ship alone. The space program, let alone the government, would not agree to allowing a lone astronaut to fly a several-billion-dollar investment. But he did not get approval. Instead, he has, in no uncertain terms, hijacked the ship, without anyone's knowledge. Yesterday, he informed the colonizers and skeleton crew, the mission would be halted for one month, that they were not to be on this initial launch, that the orders came from the top brass, and that no one was to speak of it to anyone—not even each other. They'd all be re-situated in a month's time. He lied, of course.

Harris and Waltz were the only ones informed otherwise…and however misinformed, they were now sitting in their seats at Mission Control, unknowingly helping Bing pull off the crime of the century.

"Let's not waste any more time and get this show on the road."Bing demands, annoyed.

Harris looks at Waltz, who shrugs his shoulders, in a gesture of *I guess so*.

"Roger that, Civitas I," Harris concedes, "Confirming your readiness for initiation of launch sequencing."

"Affirmative, Legion. Civitas I is ready to go."

"Copy that. You are now T-minus five. Please verify all manual controls are set and in their proper positions."

"Manual controls are set, double-checked, and in their proper positions."

"Civitas I, you are T-minus one and set for takeoff."

"Roger that. We are a go for launch."

Bing sits back and closes his eyes, pleased with himself and how he has fooled everyone. Soon, he will be the leader of a brand-new world.

"10, 9, 8, 7, 6, 5, 4, 3, 2, 1…Liftoff!

NIGHTMARES

Dappled light washes over Young Bobbie and the Elder as they sit under the shade of the moss-covered oaks. Bobbie listens to the Elder, clinging to the words of the parental figure she so desperately needs, not understanding why her parents were taken away from her.

"You are special, Little Moonstone. You always have been. Your parents have been summoned to another place. You will see In'a and A'a again, one day. Remember, I told you, they are a part of everything that surrounds you. You will always carry them in your heart, in your soul. For your soul is a part of everything, and everything is a part of your soul. Close your eyes. Feel the ground underneath you, feel how you are one with the earth." Bobbie closes her eyes, comforted by the stable ground under her. "Do you feel the strength of Mother Earth supporting you?"

"Yes."

"Imagine yourself among the stars. Imagine Father Moon shining his light upon you."

Bobbie doesn't imagine the moon or the stars. She sees her father, her real father, his stone held high to the heavens.

"I don't see the moon. I just see Papa." She opens her eyes.

"You will learn, in time. You must look deep inside yourself. You were born with the gifts to heal this world."

"What can I do to heal the world? I'm just a girl, just an orphan. I'm nothing special."

"You are not an orphan. You are part of this Nation, as you are Caddo. You also belong to Mother Earth and Father Moon. And you carry knowledge and strength beyond your wildest dreams. You will heal others. You will learn, in time, what you must do. You will learn, in time, that you have family, that you are a part of a people with special gifts. Your earthly parents were here to form you, to guide you, to lead you to us."

"But, how will I learn? How will I know?"

"You will follow your heart, Little Moonstone, you will hear its voice. And when all is quiet, your dreams will guide

you."

"My dreams are scary."

"They frighten you because you don't understand them. Don't fear them, follow them."

"How, Elder?"

"You will know."

"When? When will I know?"

"When you wake up...WAKE UP!"

THE GREAT ECAPE

With a sharp breath, Bobbie's eyes open to a wash of morning light breaking through the misshapen lid of the dumpster. The sliver of sunlight illuminates her irises, shining like blue topaz gemstones seen under a jeweler's loop, while the rest of her face sits in darkness. Her lids flutter as a shadow breaks the light above and talons click on metal. Bobbie lets out a soft moan, regaining her wits, her mind trying to make sense of where she is. She can see the pale yellow eye of the bird as it curiously peeps into the crack of the lid. *Where am I?*

Her senses slowly awaken and she is overcome by an odor, the stench rancid. She eyes the metal walls of the dumpster and weakly pushes herself up onto her side. The shock of pain in her left shoulder makes her nauseous. She heaves bile into a dry mouth and spits. She wipes her mouth on her tank top and looks down at her shoulder, where two pink circles sit, surrounded by crusty blood. Talons click upon the metal above. The smell inside the dumpster is overwhelming. She needs to get out. She pushes herself up to sitting as her eyes adjust to her dark environment, revealing her situation, sat atop a mass of paper—the paper, missing persons fliers, coated in blood. She feels something soft, yet firm, underneath her. Then she sees it, the petrified face of General Saltzman, bullet hole in his forehead, eyes wide open. She screams and the bird flies off as Bobbie scrambles backward to the other end of the dumpster, away from the dead general.

It all rushes back to her, like a punch in the gut—the general, Bing, Morris, the gunshots. She inspects her shoulder again, pushes her fingers into her pink skin. *Where are the holes?*

She has been thrown into a metal coffin like a piece of garbage. She realizes they must think she's dead, and now she needs to escape before anyone is the wiser. She pushes up on the lid of the dumpster, just a bit, and peeks out. She sees an incinerator in the distance, and a forklift carries an empty dumpster heading her way. She crouches back inside, trying not to look at the general, but the sun through the pinhole, reflecting off his glaring glass eye makes it hard for her to look away. Then she notices her abandoned backpack and grabs it. How is she going to slip away when every entrance and exit is locked and guarded?

The forklift rumbles as it nears, slamming the empty dumpster down and spearing the one next to hers. It backs up slowly and then drives off to the incinerator to dump its contents. It's only a matter of time until it returns for hers. What is she going to do? She hears the tick tick tick of the general's antique watch, alerting her she has only seconds to make a decision. His glass eye glistens in the light…and therein lies her answer. Swallowing the rancid taste in her mouth, she places her backpack on and nears the general. He's stiff as a board as she crawls over his body, dry heaving at the thought. Her hand trembles as she reaches, horrified at what she is about to do. Fingers in his eye socket, she grabs hold of of the marble. She gags as she pulls it out.

She hears the bang of the other dumpster in the distance as the forklift empties its contents into the incinerator. *It's now or never.* She opens the lid, hoists herself up, and falls to the ground…then, she runs like hell.

NO ONE'S HOME

Bobbie peers out from her hiding spot, wedged within a group of large metal barrels. She slowly shifts position, careful to not make any noise or sudden movements, so as not to draw the attention of the guard in the distance. She can't help but fidget as cramps grip her legs from being crouched for too long. That and the overwhelming smell of crude oil makes her dizzy and agitated. She takes in her surroundings, she's in some type of back area, behind Sky Ranch, the perimeter enclosed by a chain link fence topped with razor wire, separating her from the mountains beyond. She impatiently waits for the right time to run, to escape into the clearing and disappear into the mountains. She longs to stretch her legs so badly, but she can't—the guard patrolling the exit has not left his shift in quite some time.

She rubs her fingers along her aching shoulder, over the two pink scars that were once holes, then she feels behind her shoulder, and the two bumps there as well. Her mind flashes back to the spark from the gun barrel and the projectiles moving toward her in slow motion. The bullets must have gone straight through. But, how is she not dead? She was, after all, left abandoned, bleeding out in a dumpster. And how is she healed?

Weak and dizzy, her anxiety courses through, as she worries about escaping this god-forsaken place, wondering how she will ever get past the guard. She unconsciously traces an infinity sign in the dirt, a mindless habit now, acting out the repetitive motion of the soothing shape. She notices the gathering ants following her lead, traveling within the shape. She grows the shape, longer, wider, and again, even more ants follow the path she imprints in the earth.

She looks at the ants and then to the guard, positioned close by. *I am either crazy, or this is going to work.* With four fingers, she changes her pattern, brushing the dirt away from her, in four straight lines—away from her, and toward the guard. She imagines the ants follow the four lines and travel directly to him.

And, just like that, they've read her mind—just like she thought they did when she was a kid, and obediently travel in four straight lines, across the way. Over time, they are up the boots, and into the pant legs of the guard. At first, he shakes a leg at the annoyance, not really knowing what is going on. Then, he sees the ants on the ground—thousands of them, on his boots, on his pants. He brushes his legs, hopping around, trying to get the ants off him. It's overwhelming, the tickle of the insects crawling inside his clothes, in his shirt, up his neck, and into his ears. He runs off, slapping himself, ducking into the nearest building, leaving his post behind

With no time to waste, Bobbie sneaks over to the locked gate and fishes the general's eye out of her pants pocket, holding it up to the circular pad near the door. A laser scans it but nothing happens. She tries again, adjusting the marble so the iris is lined up with the center of the circle. Once again, a laser scans it and, this time, the gate unlocks. Bobbie runs through on weak legs—all pins and needles from no circulation. But at least she is free—for the moment. She needs to find shelter far away from Sky Ranch.

Under the shade of a juniper tree, Bobbie rummages through her backpack until she finds her phone, which is about to die. Grateful for a slice of battery life, she opens her settings to change her voicemail. "This is Dr. Bobbie Ann Broadbent. I am lost in the mountains of Sedona, Arizona. I was taken to a facility called Sky Ranch. I don't know exactly where I am, or the name of the mountain range, but my last photo in the cloud will be my perspective." She then takes a panoramic shot of the mountain she sees in front of her.

Battery dwindling, she opens her contacts in search of Noah's number. She's going to need his help to get out of there. She scrolls through the N's then the S's, but there is no contact card for Noah Springfield. She doesn't understand what's happening—she's sure she had him programmed into her phone and desperately needs to speak to him. He's the only one who will know how to find her.

Instead, Bobbie dials a number—one from memory, the one she knew when she was a kid, the one to his house in

Uncertain. She dials, not expecting anyone to answer. The phone rings and an older woman answers.

“Hello?”

“Hello? Mrs Springfield?” Bobbie hasn’t heard Noah’s mother’s voice in thirty years.

“Yes, this is she. Who’s asking?”

“Mrs. Springfield, this is Bobbie Ann Broadbent.” Silence. Bobbie looks at her phone to see if she is still connected.

“Oh! Bobbie Ann. My goodness. It’s been years, dear. How nice of you to call.”

“I was wondering if you had Noah’s cell number. It’s urgent I speak with him.” Silence again. “Mrs. Springfield?”

“Oh, dear. You haven’t heard?”

“Haven’t heard what?”

“Can’t imagine you would’ve, being they whisked you away so quickly after your momma passed. You’ve been gone so long.”

“What haven’t I heard, Mrs. Springfield?”

"Heard about my boy, Noah." The woman's voice cracks.

Bobbie is confused, she asks again, "What haven't I heard about Noah?"

"Noah died, Bobbie Ann."

Bobbie's blood runs cold. "What! When?"

"It's been almost thirty years now."

"But I…I was just…"

"He drowned, dear. In Caddo Lake."

"Drowned?"

"They never did find my baby's body. Just his empty boat."

Bobbie hears the quiet sobs of a mother grieving the loss of a son like it was yesterday.

"I'm so sorry, Mrs. Springfield."

Bobbie hangs up, dazed, staring at her dirty pant legs, crusted over with dried blood and desert soot. On her phone's browser she searches *Noah Springfield, Uncertain Texas*, and scrolls through the results. There is no profile for a military man.

There are no journalistic entries into any type of publication. His name is not listed as one of the most recent Nobel Prize recipients. There is only one entry, an article from a local paper about a missing boy, who paddled out, onto Caddo Lake in his little red rowboat, and is believed to have drowned. There is no other article of any Lieutenant Noah Springfield, and there won't be because the screen on her phone is black, emblazoned with the symbol of an empty battery. She sets it aside. Numb. Not knowing what is reality. She reaches into her backpack and slowly pulls out the crumpled envelope Noah gave her. The one with the notes for her speech. The one she never looked at because she was in a hurry, because she'd figured out, on her own, what she was going to say. She removes the folded paper tucked into the envelope and opens it. The paper is blank.

ALONE AGAIN

Bobbie hugs her hoodie around herself, pulling it over her bare legs crouched into her as she sits, shivering in the night, taking shelter on a ledge of the abandoned dwelling carved into the side of the mountain. It took all she had to hike to the spot, trying to make sense of the new of Noah, looking behind her the whole way, making sure no one discovered and captured her. But why would they? For all they knew, she was dead. She and the general, incinerated after being murdered. She wondered if the whole establishment was corrupt. Then again, General Saltzman didn't seem to know or approve of what Bing was up to. Maybe no one else did either. Maybe it was only Bing and his henchman who were evil-doers.

She hated Bing and his plan to obliterate a whole civilization, in order to colonize a planet. She hated the fact he had control over the narrative of her vaccine, that he could pull the wool over the unsuspecting eyes of the public and make it seem that her discovery was bad when it was actually *his* mutant iteration that was destructive. All she wanted to do was save people, to help them not suffer from the horrible thing that took her mother away from her at such a young age. That's all she wanted to do…save people.

Bobbie feels weak. Her wound, although healed from the outside, sends shooting pain through her shoulder. And she is thirsty…so thirsty, her mouth feels dried with cotton balls and dusted with earth. She lies on the ground, folded like a pillbug, backpack as her pillow, and closes her eyes, drifting off into a fitful sleep.

NIGHTMARES

A child once again, Bobbie stands among the glowing anemone, lulled by the peaceful shush and whoosh of their motion. The feeling is different this time. She is not searching for a way out, for she is tired. Tired of running. This time, she welcomes the uncertainty, willing to face whatever it is that stands beyond the void.

"Bobbie Ann." Her father stands in front of her, urgency in his eyes, holding his moonstone out toward her. She reaches, but she can't grab it, as if an impenetrable forcefield divides them. "Alter his course, Bobbie Ann."

"Whose Papa?"

"Use your gift. They are here, they will help you."

"Who will help me, Papa?"

Her father slowly backs away, disappearing into the anemone. "Use your gift."

"Papa, wait!"

"Alter his course." His message trails off.

"Papa!"

BEAMS OF LIGHT

Bobbie shouts herself awake calling for her father, and jumps to her feet in mad frustration. Fatherless and motherless, this defiant orphan balls her fists and looks toward the heavens, in order to curse Father Moon.

Instead, she draws in a breath, awestruck at the pitch-black sky. It's exquisite. She can see every star in the universe, clearer than ever, twinkling brighter than ever, with no artificial light to dull their shine. She can see the Milky Way and every constellation, plain as day, outlined as if someone connected their dots with a white sharpie. Ursas Major, and Minor, the Big and Little Dipper, and especially Orion, the Hunter. Orion—with the extra star in his belt—the one bigger than the others—the one she now knows as Hesperus.

"You know, you've got to move that planet," a familiar voice calls from behind.

Bobbie spins around, scared half to death. "Noah?" She rubs her eyes, not believing what she sees.

Noah stands, an apparition of himself. "Move the

planet," he says once again, smiling warmly, before dissipating into a thousand twinkling fireflies.

"Noah! Noah, don't go!" she cries, reaching out, as the tiny lighted insects scatter into the night. "Aargh!" she shouts, frustrated by the messages of her father and Noah, who've abandoned her once again. "Alter his course! Move the planet!" she screams into the void like a madwoman, falling to her knees with despair. The darkness answers as her screams echo back to her from the canyons. *Alter his course, move the planet, alter his course.* She hears the connected phrases. *Move the planet, alter his course.* "But, how can I move a planet?" She sobs to no-one.

Defeated, she covers her face with her hands, crying rivers of tears that streak her sooty skin like shooting stars across the sky. Under the moonlight, her ring becomes energized. The moonstone glows brightly, sending a vibration down her finger, causing her to stare at the beautiful stone. She can hear the Elder's voice clearly. *"This belongs to you, Little Moonstone, was meant for you. One day, you will help the great Star People.*

Today is that day."

Bobbie wipes away her tears and rushes to her backpack, rummaging through to find her father's moonstone. If here phone weren't dead, she'd notice the time was 3:00 A.M.

Guided by instinct, she stands at the edge of the cliff and raises the stone over her head with both hands, like she'd seen her father do all those years ago. She has no idea what she's doing. Maybe she's gone crazy, delirious with exhaustion; her brain dehydrated, parched and cracked like the desert. She doesn't care. She draws in a long breath and grounds herself, kicking off her shoes, digging her feet into the dust, and exhaling ever so calmly. She feels stable Mother Earth Beneath her, supporting her efforts. Bobbie imagines her feet growing roots, reaching deep into the ground, planting herself firmly, giving her strength.

Under the light of the moon, the stone begins to glow. Bobbie looks up to the heavens and whispers, "Father Moon," to the bright, cratered mass hanging above her, charging the stone, which vibrates in her hands. Bobbie stumbles back, not expecting the forceful energy, as the moonstone emits a beam up into the sky. She digs her feet back into the dry earth, regaining her connection. But, nothing else happens. Her beam is beaming, but the planet doesn't move, it doesn't even wobble. She wonders if it's because there is no circle of burning sage on the ground around her. *What am I doing?* She begins to doubt herself.

Bobbie wonders if maybe she's mentally ill, and this is all just one giant hallucination. How could someone move a planet with a beautiful rock? How could Noah be here one day and gone the next? Maybe she did die, and this is purgatory.

Still, she is unable to quit. *Alter his course.* Her arms feel supported by some unknown force; like she's not in charge, like something is pulling them, magnetically drawing them upward, the way she was pulled toward the lights when she was a child. Her shoulder aches, damaged by greed and fear and burdened with the weight of the world. But the stone stays high.

As she stares at the sky, waiting for something to happen,

tears fall back from her eyes, triggered by the memories of Noah, of her father, and especially her mother. Even the Elder is no longer. Why is she alone in this world? Why does she have no one? Suddenly, from behind, a swirly iridescent beam of light shoots over her head and intertwines with hers. Then another, and another—like shooting stars, they fly over her head and through the sky, interweaving with each other, braiding themselves together as one, gaining strength in numbers, growing longer and larger, until they become one giant, beam. The immense power in Bobbie's palms reverberates throughout her whole body.

She has her eye on Orion's belt, on Hesperus specifically, and on the great plaited beam pointed at it. And like a punch to its gut, the star flickers, then shrinks, becoming much smaller than the others, positioning itself to a different point in the galaxy. Bobbie marvels at the beam and what it has accomplished, as it slowly begins to unravel. Each entwined ray, disengaging itself and becoming individual once more, traveling back to where it originated—behind Bobbie. Her own stone follows suit, sucking its power back into itself, leaving her standing on the ledge of a mountain in complete silence. She lets out the breath she'd been holding and places her hand over her heart, feeling different, as if somehow the crater of loneliness was now full and overflowing.

Bobbie slowly turns to look behind her, to see just where the light beams originated. She gasps at the sight. One hundred Sinagua have emerged from the holes in the side of the mountain, all lowering their moonstones from the sky. In the middle of the pack—her father.

LIFTOFF

Legion flight controllers Waltz and Harris scramble to command the Mission Control desk by themselves, while Bing is projected onto a fifty-foot screen in front of them. He is strapped into his captain's chair, hurtling through space and headed toward Hesperus.

"Civitas I to Mission Control," Bing calls, buckled in for the long haul.

"Roger, Civitas," Harris answers. "You're loud and clear. We've got you on visuals."

"All set for Hesperus, course is steady, and ready for final thrust."

"Roger that. Final thrust has been configured. Stand by."

"Roger."

A small glitch interrupts the transmission on the screen.

"Enable ignition," instructs Harris.

"Ignition enabled," Bing replies, his words stuttered.

The video hiccups, distorting the image. Waltz covers his mic and turns to Harris. "What's going on?"

Harris presses buttons on the equipment. “I have no idea.”

“Ignition enabled-ed-ed,” Bing repeats.

“Roger that, Civitas I, hold tight.”

Bing’s face, static on the frozen screen, is distorted—pixelated into an abstract pattern, as buzzing sound overtakes the comms. The engineers attempt a response from their equipment, trying to get ahold of why their visuals are glitching and how they can fix it. Suddenly an alarm sounds, ringing through the empty control room. The video of Bing continues to cut in and out, alternating between a moving image and a static one, as Harris and Waltz scramble from one desk to another.

“I told you we needed a team!” Waltz barks, frustrated.

“We couldn’t!” Harris fires back. “Commander’s orders. The mission is covert.”

“Legion…what’s…on down there?” Bings transmission is choppy.

‘Hold tight, Civitas I,” Harris instructs as he tinkers.

"There seems to be a slight problem."

"A pro…em?" Bing asks.

"Let's switch to autopilot," Waltz suggests to Harris.

"Okay," responds Harris. "Go check the motherboard."

Waltz pulls off his headset and hurries to another room to check the brain of the equipment as the video continues to malfunction.

"Legion to Civitas I, we're going to lock in autopilot."

"Rog…tha…"

"Autopilot engaged. Final destination, Hesperus."

"Rog…"

"Waltz, c'mon back, I need your help," Harris calls over the intercom as he reviews the flight path. "Waltz," he calls again, pressing buttons on Waltz's console, juggling the job of two men. "Wait a damn minute…" his face turns ashen, "something's off…Waltz!" He hollers, frantically adjusting his equipment.

Waltz arrives back to his position, sweating, looking a bit

dazed.

“We’ve got a problem,” Harris tells him. “These coordinates are way off, and he’s on autopilot. I can’t get the equipment to respond. Dammit! We need to change these coordinates ASAP.” He adjusts settings to no avail. “Civitas I, come in.”

Bing’s distorted face is frozen on screen as static hisses over the comms.

“Why, what’s wrong with the coordinates?” asks an ashen Waltz.

“They are way off.” Harris stares at his monitors in disbelief. “It looks like the fucking planet has moved!”

Waltz closes his eyes and lowers his head.

“Waltz! Let’s get a move on!” Harris demands. “With these coordinates, he’s set to hurtle directly into a black hole. We’ll never be able to retrieve the ship. Let’s get this fucking equipment working!”

“We can’t.”

“We can’t what?”

“Get the equipment working.”

“Why the hell not?”

“The motherboard is fried.”

Harris pulls off his comms and turns to his partner. “What the fuck are you talking about?”

“The motherboard is gone. Destroyed. Corroded.”

“Corroded with what?”

“Ants. Millions of them.”

NOT THIS TIME

Bobbie emerges from a steamy shower and wraps herself in a terry robe. Meditation music plays throughout her apartment as she squeezes a dab of toothpaste onto a toothbrush and begins to brush. She wipes condensation from the mirror with one hand, brushing in circular motions with the other. She spits and replaces her toothbrush to its holder.

She pulls her robe away from her shoulder and stares at the reflection of the triangular scar beneath her clavicle. With new perspective, she touches it, appreciating it, then moves to her other shoulder, to the two scars from the bullet wounds. The mirror has steamed again, and again she wipes the condensation away. Her stomach drops. Morris stands behind her.

Bobbie screams and Morris lunges toward her grabbing her by the shoulders. They struggle and he pushes her up against a counter, trying to squeeze her neck in between his hands. She fumbles behind herself, patting the counter top, looking for anything to use as a weapon. She grabs a perfume bottle and sprays the liquid into Morris's eyes. He hollers, wiping his eyes, and she runs into her living room.

"Nimbus, summon the police!"

"Summoning the police."

An alarm sounds as Bobbie races to her front door. Morris catches up to her and pulls her back into her apartment by her hair. They struggle. He slams her up against the glass wall of ants. The ants appear agitated. They swarm together, like a black cloud toward Bobbie's attacker as she tries to pry Morris's tight grip from her throat. She knees him hard in the groin. He doubles over, holding his crotch with one hand and leaning on the wall of ants with the other.

Bobbie pulls a plug from the ant farm, making a large space for the ants to escape. They quickly swarm onto Morris' hand and up his arm stinging him along the way. They are all over him, hundreds of ants, as he spins and screams, trying to remove his clothes, trying to brush them off. The small creatures are relentless, as they continually inject their poison into his skin, defending their owner.

Bobbie tightens her robe as she watches Morris fall to the floor, gasping, writhing, and foaming from the mouth, as her protective ants devour him, leaving only a remnant of the man he once was.

BYE-BYE BING

Somewhere in space…

Bing, alone on his ship and in a panic, hurtles to nowhere, unsuccessfully adjusting settings, trying to alter his course to no avail.

"Civitas I to Mission Control…Legion, come in… Legion, can you hear me?" There is nothing but static—static over silence. "Aargh!"

He unbuckles himself, like a maniac, and moves to the small window, peering out into the void, knowing he's a goner. With a path to oblivion and no communications with Earth, it's only a matter of time until Bing runs out of food and water. Until he runs out of oxygen. The kicker is, he's injected himself with POH Plus, so he won't die, not quickly anyway. He can survive in an oxygen-less environment. So, he will live every second of every minute of every week, month and year of his life, suffering. Replaying the movie in his head, wondering where it all went wrong. Civitas I will be his final resting place. A metal coffin in the sky—until it is sucked into a black hole and violently implodes, pulverizing its passenger.

As Bing ponders his doom, a shadow crosses his face. Something is outside. “Hey!” He yells, face close to the porthole, fogging it with desperate breath, trying to get the attention of the colossal airship in the distance. “Heeyyy!” He shouts, wiping his breath off the glass to get a better look.

The craft grows massive as it slowly nears, moaning, ominously looming overhead, dwarfing Bing’s ship: like a whale to a minnow. One thousand miles wide.

“Hey!” Bing howls, as he slaps the window, trying to make out the red call numbers on the colossal vessel.

The gargantuan ship ignores the desperate man as it slowly passes over, a creaking billboard, it’s silvery body emblazoned with the letters NOHS-RK.

From the outside looking in, the porthole frames the pained face of the stranded astronaut. Like a portrait—a living, breathing portrait of a petrified man, mouth open wide, howling in terror.

But there is no sound to be heard.

Because in space, no one can hear you scream.

EPILOGUE

Bobbie looks out onto Caddo Lake, wrapped in a small outer-space blanket, the old house she shared with her mother in the distance behind her. A thick mist hovers above the water's surface and gentle ripples lap against the shore—a familiar tempo from a time long ago. It's been months since her escape from Sky Ranch and the attempt on her life by wayward agent Morris: the only way to silence her and her knowledge of the ranch. After a long series of clandestine interviews and government investigations, the program at Sky Ranch was shut down, and all remnants of POH Plus destroyed—all bad actors sent to prison.

Bobbie's vaccine was approved and continues to work as intended, saving lives. She was awarded the Presidential Medal of Honor for her service in helping humankind.

She now heads up another program in the old Sky Ranch facility, working alongside other scientists and historians, studying and preserving the cliff dwellings created by the long forgotten Sinagua, and facilitating a program unearthing their connection to the Star People.

The cliff dwelling has been deemed a national monument, and the mountains part of the national parks system. The culture and history are to be studied, protected, and preserved—to be written about for generations to come. Both on Earth, and in space. When asked about the rumblings of possible alien life on Hesperus: Bobbie has no comment.

A *thunk* joins the rhythm of the water, and Bobbie walks closer to its edge to investigate. Something protrudes—a petrified piece of wood with an acorn finial. She can't believe her eyes. Her old ant farm, smashed and battered, emerges from the sludge at the shore, as if it was just recently tossed there by her bully. She leans down and takes ahold of it, swishing what's left of it from side to side, cleaning the mud from its base. The glass is all but gone, but the frame is still intact, albeit askew, as it has seen better days. Bobbie shakes off the water and smiles. With a little elbow grease and some new glass panels, she's sure she can bring this precious memento back to life. *It will look worse for the wear, but don't we all.*

The cry of a hawk from the clouds above distracts her. She watches as it circles in the sky, graceful and choreographed, making a figure eight, swooping closer and closer to the water, then closer and closer to her, seemingly connecting the two with its invisible path, until it's almost upon her. It sweeps past her, close enough for her to feel the wind from its handsome wings. It flies over her, then back over the water, skimming the calm surface with its talons, plucking a fish up into the air and taking it back to its nest in the forest. The ripples left in the water expand and disappear into the mist, where the bow of a small red boat slowly emerges. Bobbie catches her breath at the sight of the boat's captain. It's Noah, as a boy, standing in his tiny ark. An all-to-real apparition. He raises a hand and smiles.

For a moment, Bobbie is ten again, wrapped in her outer-space blanket, wild hair blowing in the wind, holding her ant farm. She raises a hand and smiles back at Noah, who dissipates into the mist, along with his boat.

She hugs her blanket tighter, tears in her eyes at the memory of her only friend. The squeal of worn brakes behind her pulls her focus. A moving van maneuvers into the driveway of her childhood home. A man hops out and pulls open the van's back doors, revealing a floor to ceiling ant farm.

Bobbie smiles and and walks toward her old home, soon to be new once again.

THANK YOU READERS, for taking time out of your lives to read Bobbie's Ants. Without you, an author's words would never be seen and our magical worlds would never be lived. You give validation to our imaginations and I am more than grateful for that.

I also want to thank my friend Robert Paschall Jr., who has no idea that his suggestion brought this story to life. While I was trying to pitch the screenplays of my other two books for him to produce, in the kindest rejection ever, he explained to me that I was writing features (they were too long) and that I should write a one-hour action flick instead. So I started developing a screenplay for a one hour action flick about outer space. Unfortunately, I hated every minute of it, because that wasn't my genre and I struggled through every scene, not knowing where the story was going, trying to come up with some kind of plot with which I had no experience. But something happened in the middle of it….I surrendered. I realized I loved the character of Bobbie Ann Broadbent, and that her story would make for an amazing book. I could see Bobbie, down to her last freckle. I could hear her, feel her emotions, and I wanted to know how her life experience would unfold. So I started writing the opening scene and Bobbie's Ants developed easily from there.

I'd also like to thank my friend Antonia "Ant" Reed, whose generous stories, and life experience gave me something to grasp on to, embellish, and express—all with great imagination.

BE KIND: to each other, to nature, to creatures both big and small. For, if we stop and notice the world—really notice—we will recognize that we are not alone, and that every living thing has a soul and is a gift unto us. The symbolism of Bobbie watching the ants in her farm correlates to the universe watching humans on the planet. There is always something bigger out there.

Cherie Fruehan was born and raised in Scranton, Pennsylvania. She is an author and artist who earned her BFA from Marywood University. As a member of MENSA, her artwork has been published on both the covers and inside pages of the MENSA bulletin.

Read Cherie's other books: Dinner With The Hawthornes and The Suicide of Sophie Rae

Socials: @cheriefruehan

Website: www.cheriefruehan.com

www.ingramcontent.com/pod-product-compliance
Lightning Source LLC
La Vergne TN
LVHW041106080826
845145LV00007B/1706

* 9 7 8 1 7 3 4 6 1 4 1 4 5 *